AUG - 2017

QUEEN OF THE CROWS

HARMONY WAGNER

D1315524

© 2016

All rights reserved. No part of this publication may be reproduced, stored in a retrieval system, or transmitted, in any form or by any means, without the prior written permission of the publisher or, in case of photocopying or other reprographic copying, a licence from the Canadian Copyright Licensing Agency.

ACORNPRESS

P.O. Box 22024
Charlottetown, Prince Edward Island
C1A 9J2
acornpresscanada.com

Edited by Penelope Jackson
Copy edit by Laurie Brinklow
Cover and poster design by Jason Rogerson
Layout and feather illustration by Matt Reid
Photography by PixbyLorne
Printed in Canada

Library and Archives Canada Cataloguing in Publication

Wagner, Harmony, author
Queen of the crows / Harmony Wagner.

Based on short film with same name.
Issued in print and electronic formats.
ISBN 978-1-927502-68-6 (paperback).--ISBN 978-1-927502-73-0 (html)

I. Title.

PS8645.A385Q44 2016   jC813'.6   C2016-906470-0
                                               C2016-906471-9

The publisher acknowledges the support of the Government of Canada through the Canada Book Fund of the Department of Canadian Heritage and the Canada Council for the Arts Block Grant Program and the support of the Province of Prince Edward Island.

for A.V.R

CHAPTER 1

Caw! Caw!

Crows darted and flapped outside the window, waking Elsa at dawn.

She tried to sense the presence of someone else in the house. It felt still and empty.

Elsa crept down the hall and glanced down the stairs. No shoes by the door. She simultaneously felt relief and despair. Sometimes, when she saw her mother's high heels sprawled there, accompanied by a pair of big boots, she knew not to continue down the hall.

But with no shoes there at all, there was still hope. She crept quietly towards her mother's door and peeked around. The messy bed was still empty. The weight of the situation pulled down on her heart, pushing out a loud sigh. Elsa quietly made the bed.

Her mother had been gone for four days now. It wasn't the first time she had disappeared, though no one else knew that. But this was the longest she had ever been gone. Elsa had managed to go to school and act normal, but sooner or later she knew someone would figure out what was going on, and then what? She wasn't willing to find out.

The dim light outside cast a grey-blue shade over the kitchen. Elsa pulled the empty peanut butter jar down from the cupboard and scraped the last bits out with a spoon. She opened the fridge. The harsh glare of light hurt her eyes.

A dilapidated bread bag and egg carton sat lonely in the otherwise empty, dirty fridge. She ceremoniously pulled her last meal out onto the counter. With no butter or oil left for scrambled, she put on a little pot of water to poach the egg. As she waited, she fished into the bowels of the bag. After three days of eating only two eggs and a piece of bread per day, she was down to the two sad-looking heel-ends of the loaf.

Out in the yard there was a flurry of black in the grey morning.

Caw! Caw! Caw! Caw!

Three big crows swooped and darted at a small, mangy-looking crow that had landed with a pizza crust in its beak. The big crows pecked at the small crow to steal the prize.

Caw! Caw! Wings flapped and black bodies bounced around in the light snow.

"Hey!" shouted Elsa as she opened the back door. A big crow snatched up the pizza crust and flew off. The others followed, leaving the sad little crow looking at her with a tilt of his head.

"Sorry," she said, her skin bracing at the cold late November air. "I was just trying to help."

The crow looked straight at her. Its head tilted again slightly. Elsa looked down at the two bread rinds in her hands.

"Here." She gently tossed a piece towards the crow. She'd never loved the crusts anyway, especially not the cheap white spongy kind. The awkward shape of the bread wobbled in the wind and didn't make it past the deck.

Elsa closed the door and dropped her egg in the boiling water. She put her heel of bread in the toaster. She knew she was going to be hungry either way, so why not help out a fellow straggler? The crow gazed cautiously through the glass of the door, then hopped up onto the stairs of the deck and pecked voraciously at the bread.

Elsa sat at the little kitchen table dipping her dry toast into the warm gooiness of the egg. She finished up her homework assignment, slowly chewing the precious bites of her meagre breakfast. Her heart lifted a little bit watching the crow gulp down her gift. But she sighed at the thought of the day ahead of her.

In addition to food, she was out of clean clothes. She hunted the couch, cupboards, and her mother's dresser for any stash spots of spare change. Nothing.

She needed money for the laundromat. She knew coming to school in the same old dirty clothes might tip off the adults that something was up. Not that Mom actually did the laundry. Elsa had been handling that, the shopping, and pretty much everything else since she was nine. As she rooted through her mother's drawers, she knew she had to do her best to keep a low profile. She was playing the long game. She could do this. And Mom would be back. Eventually.

It was always a double-edged sword when Mom returned. For a while there would be a flurry of hugs, compliments, rambunctious adventures, maybe even some ridiculous gifts they couldn't afford and then...the crash. Elsa longed for those little windows of happy attention. But she also knew they came with a cost. Mom would soon be flat in her bed staring at the wall. Elsa would know where she was, but she didn't really get to have her, just the shape of a body under those messy blankets.

Elsa sifted through the shirts in the drawer. Most of them were obviously too big or too sexy for an eleven-year-old. She shut the drawer with a thud. Then she spied a bulging plastic bag from a thrift store in the corner of the room. She dumped it out onto the bed and rummaged through the clothes.

Mom spending money they didn't have was always one of the signs that she was going to go on an upswing. So was her provocative dressing. Elsa batted aside a bunch of lacey leopardskin stuff and saw an orange-and-white striped shirt with a little blue anchor on the chest. Under that was a small pair of cotton lavender pants. She felt a flicker of delight that Mom had been thinking of her, too, as she tried them on. The pants were a little tight, but they would have to do. She took off the shirt to cut off the price tag. It still smelled like a thrift store, but it was better than the ketchup- and grass-stained options in her room. She slipped it back on and looked at herself in her mother's mirror. She could almost see her future woman self, about to push out from under her skin.

As hard as this had been, she felt proud of what she had accomplished so far. Now it was time to get outside. She still had an hour before school and she had work to do.

With her last big blue plastic bag in hand, she locked the front door.

Caw! A crow cawed from the tree across the street.

Elsa looked up to see the crow spread open its wings as it clutched the branch. Two feathers were missing from its right wing.

I wonder if it's the same crow?

Elsa gave it a little smile and a small tilt of her head.

Crllllll, chirped the bird.

Elsa had always wondered what it meant when crows made that throat-rolling sound. Maybe it meant "thanks." She smirked and warmed a little from the thought as she tucked her cold bare hands into the sleeves of her jacket.

One of Elsa's tricks was waking early and collecting returnable bottles and cans from the public trash cans on the way to and from school. She always went through the park near her house first. There were lots of spots where she could collect without anyone seeing her, and she was keenly aware that staying under the radar was in her best interest.

Her mother didn't do well with parent-teacher interviews. Over the years there had been plenty of visits from cops, social workers, and psychologists, all asking Elsa leading questions, and she knew where they headed: being separated from her mom. Dana wasn't the most perfect woman in the world, but Elsa burned with anger at the thought that strangers could take away her own mother.

She checked over her shoulder and then stuffed a few pop cans into her bag. The crows cawed loudly in the trees overhead as the sun burst out from behind the low clouds on the horizon.

Elsa loved this park. The river, the trees, and the thousands of crows that roosted in them over the winter. This was the place where she felt at home. Where she felt peace.

After visiting all her usual trashcans, her bag was a quarter full. Normally, she would stash it in the woods and then check them all again on the way home from school. But desperate times called for desperate measures. She decided to carry on closer to school to see if she could find a bit more so she would be able to cash it in after school. A stuffed-to-the-gills bag was worth around five dollars. And she wanted to eat something other than bread and eggs tonight.

She took the quietest path she could think of. Small neighbourhood streets with as little car traffic as possible. The last thing she needed was a teacher or classmate to drive by and see her picking through the garbage.

She knew it was recycling day on Thursdays starting on Garden Street. She scurried to find pay dirt. Garden Street was lined with blue bags in front of every house. It was a run-down side street in a low-income neighbourhood. She knew no one would bat an eye at her picking through the recycling. Unfortunately, people in this neighbourhood often kept their returnables so they could cash them in themselves.

The sun was already high and the city was waking up so she worked quickly, scanning the bags that had the most valuable containers. She opened a few and fished through the bag for various things of value. Pop cans, beer cans, juice cartons, bottles of all sorts. On high alert, she winnowed through, trying not to get dirty. Also, she had seen hypodermic needles in a bag on this street one time.

Dana! Why do you put me through this?

Elsa worked fast, her stomach clenched. She turned her back as a car passed. Despite her high stress, she remained true to the code of all gleaners: never rip the bag. She and all the other folks who sifted through other people's recyclables for a living knew not to mess with a good thing. Ripping the bags annoyed the people who put this free money out on the streets. The cold wind bit at her hands as she worked at the knot in the plastic.

You know we're coming; why don't you just leave them open for us?!

Elsa could taste bile at the back of her throat. Was it the nerves, the hunger, or the rage? Probably all three. She stuffed her own bag full and tied it up. Now to stash it somewhere and just hope to dear god no other gleaner found it while she was stuck at school. She erased that thought. She couldn't even bear to think of it. Quickly, she scuttled across the main road and headed up to the part of Garden Street that became more industrial. She found a set of stairs in the alley behind an empty building. Looking around to see if anyone was watching, she shoved her blue bag underneath the concrete platform. She leaned a ratty old piece of plywood over it and hoped it would be there when she got back.

Without her load, Elsa could quicken her pace. She always tried to get to school early. Being late drew attention. As she neared the next main road, she saw another gleaner bent over a blue bag. The old woman looked up from her squat position and smiled with recognition.

"Hallo!" she beamed and waved her tiny little gloved hand with the fingers cut out.

Elsa's throat tightened at the realization that this was the first time anyone had smiled at her all week.

"Hello!" smiled Elsa.

The woman's beaming face brightened even more. As if she, too, was hungry for the nourishment of really being seen.

The woman was the grandmother of a Karen family that had come to the city as refugees from Burma that fall. Her grandson, Eh Ta Taw, was in Elsa's class.

They were immediately recognizable when they first arrived because, first of all, the city was small and not very multicultural. But they especially stood out to Elsa because they wore such brightly coloured clothing and walked down the road as a group in single file, with the men at the front. Another thing she had noticed immediately was how they gleaned with no shame in their hearts.

Elsa often thought about how cold and isolated they must have felt coming here. The boy in her class was so quiet and no one talked to him. A few weeks after he arrived, Elsa drew him a card with a maple leaf on it that said "Welcome to Canada," but she had been razzed to no end for having a crush on him when the mean girls found out.

Then one very windy day last month, Elsa had seen the grandmother trying to carry two very full bags of cans and bottles down the street. The tiny woman and the big bags were being blown around with such force it was almost comical. The woman was clearly unable to carry both bags into the force of the wind, but also seemed determined not to sacrifice the value of a bag by putting one down. So instead she squinted and heaved, leaning into the gusts that whipped the heavy bags around her tiny body, making very little headway at all.

Elsa ran across the street and helped carry one of the bags a few blocks to their apartment above a store. The woman had giddily tried to use the little English she knew and smiled glowingly at Elsa the whole way there. It was as if by carrying the bag, Elsa had also lifted some of the burden of being invisible.

Elsa wished she could remember the woman's name. That would have blown that beaming smile right off her head. Instead she pointed to her own chest and tapped.

"I'm Elsa."

The old woman's eyes sparkled with joy.

"My name...Pee Takaw Paw." Her smile seemed to stretch to her ears.

"Pee Takaw Paw," repeated Elsa awkwardly. She didn't pronounce it exactly right, but the woman nodded encouragingly anyway.

They beamed and waved at each other from either side of the street, eyes glistening with the joy of being acknowledged, unable to break from each other's gaze.

In the distance the school bell rang.

"Oh! I have to go to school now!

"Go school yes," the grandmother nodded warmly.

Elsa turned up the street and the woman went back to rooting through her bag. As Elsa wiped the tears from her eyes, she tried to convince herself it was just from the wind.

She sniffed her hand. It smelled garbagey. She braced against the cold as she rubbed her hands into the dusting of snow in the grass. Wiping it away, she blew on her hands to warm them. Her breath smelled like hunger and bile. She quickened her pace now, almost running to get to school on time. As she ran, she passed a cedar tree and broke off some of its leaves. She crumbled them in her hands to freshen their scent. As she neared the school she stopped at the gummy pine tree and picked off a bit of resin. She slipped it in her mouth. It tasted terrible, but she hoped the pine smell would cover the telltale scent of hunger. She rounded the corner and clambered up the stairs as the final bell rang.

Elsa struggled to quiet her breath and slow her heart as she foisted her coat into her locker.

"Try combing your hair sometime," sniffed Breagh, the leader of the mean girls. Gabby and Lenore giggled by her side as they passed in the hall.

Elsa looked in her mirror. She did look windblown. She quickly smoothed her hair and grabbed her rumpled old backpack and rushed into the class last. Ms. Witherspoon looked at the clock and watched Elsa settle into her seat. It was three past nine.

"Okay, class, let's take a look at the math assignment from yesterday."

Elsa unzipped her backpack. It was empty. The homework was still sitting on the kitchen table. Elsa's head fell into her hands. When she looked up all the other students had their assignments on their desks and Ms. Witherspoon was staring right at her.

"Is there a problem, Elsa?"

All eyes burrowed into her. Gabby and Lenore looked at Breagh with eyebrows raised. Breagh gave her famous little shoulder-bouncing sniff. Elsa tried to speak but nothing came out. She cleared her throat.

"Um, no. I just forgot it at home."

Ms. Witherspoon's gaze narrowed with disbelief. "Elsa, we have talked about this before." She placed a fresh handout firmly on the desk, with a condescending smile, and said in a shrill voice, "We are just going to have to work a little harder, aren't we?"

If only you knew how hard I work!

Elsa bit the inside of her cheeks and pushed her feelings way down. Instead of exploding, she stared blankly at the teacher because she knew it bothered her.

CHAPTER 2

Lunch hour had always been a problem. Today's was going to be especially difficult. To make things worse, at precisely 11:50 a.m., in the midst of a quiet writing assignment, Elsa's guts began not just to growl, but to howl at their emptiness.

RrrrrrRRRRRRRaaaoooollllllll!

Ms. Witherspoon looked up. Elsa sank into her seat, trying to crush her stomach into silence, burying her face in her notebook.

RRRRRReeeeeeeeoooooooooorrr.

This time the students around her couldn't help but snicker.

"Excuse me," she mumbled softly. She looked up at the clock. Nine more exhaustingly long minutes to go. The students went back to their writing.

EerrrrrrrrRRRRRRRRRRRRRrrrreeeee.

Now everyone laughed. Even Ms. Witherspoon couldn't keep a straight face.

"Everything okay, Elsa?" she asked, mostly just to settle the others.

NO. Everything is definitely NOT okay!

"I'm fine," Elsa mumbled, looking at her notebook, "but I do think I might need to use the washroom."

The whole class burst out laughing. Elsa could feel her face burst red. Tilting her head down, her thick, auburn hair surrounded her like a tent of protection.

"Class." Ms. Witherspoon frowned, but it was no use; it was too close to break time to tamp them down.

Elsa looked up without raising her face.

"Go ahead."

She grabbed her backpack and launched out of the room before her guts could betray her again. She didn't plan on going back before the noon bell rang. She would simply hang out in the washroom until it was safe to head to the library.

Elsa used this trick whenever she didn't have a lunch. Which had been fairly often over the years. She would hang out in the bathroom long enough for the librarian to think that she had wolfed her food and then she'd hang out in the library for the rest of the lunch hour to avoid the perils of the lunchroom and the schoolyard.

The lunchroom was difficult to endure without a posse. Ridicule and judgment were doled out based on the coolness factor of what you ate. Distinctions were drawn between the rich and poor, the "healthy" and the allergic, the kids who could manipulate their parents into buying the latest food status symbol and those who were stuck with whatever homemade food their parents ate. And then there was the slop from the cafeteria, which had high coolness factor, but zero nutrition. Even if Elsa had had friends, they wouldn't have eaten there.

The schoolyard was a little safer for loners if you could find a quiet zone to do your thing. The only trouble was it was also the Wild West. A few adults couldn't possibly keep tabs on a hundred kids running around and blowing off the steam that three hours of sitting in a cramped desk in a stuffy room builds up. Plus the teachers inevitably drifted into their phones or conversations with each other, leaving it open season for bullying and intimidation.

The library was quiet, peppered with a few other misfits who just wanted the peace to be who they were. Plus the librarian was cool. Probably a grown-up version of the same kind of kid, he quietly accepted anyone seeking refuge without question. After a while of unobtrusively observing what you were into reading about, he'd even introduce other cool books and links to help the hour go by.

When Elsa got to the bathroom she drank a bunch of water to soothe the angry beast. She heard someone coming so she ducked into a stall. Amidst the faded, half-scrubbed graffiti on the walls, there was fresh aquamarine ink:

Elsa's mom is nuttier than a bag of trail mix!

The *i's* had the classic hollow circle used by Breagh and imitated by Gabby and Lenore. Trusting that Breagh was too smart to risk getting caught doing graffiti, and Lenore was smart enough to not use their trademark hollow *i's*, Elsa was pretty sure that Gabby had written it.

When the coast was clear, she came out of the stall and got a huge hunk of wet paper towel and returned to scrub out the insult.

The noon bell rang. Not too long after that, the bathroom door burst open again. Suspecting who it would be, she quickly perched her feet up to squat on the toilet seat and waited. She could feel the presence of others.

They could feel hers, too. She knew they were staring at the closed stall door with no feet below.

"That's the one!" mouthed Gabby to Breagh.

"Do you think she's in there?" Lenore leaned in with a whisper.

Breagh nodded knowingly, but of course they couldn't be sure. Everyone waited in tense silence.

After a moment, Breagh blurted a taunting, "Constipated?"

Gabby and Lenore choked down their giggles, waiting to see what would happen next.

Elsa decided to call their bluff. She flushed the toilet. The girls squealed and raced out to protect their identities in case it was someone else about to step out of the stall.

Elsa stepped off the toilet and went back to scrubbing. It didn't come off easily. She pressed harder and rubbed more vigorously. As drops of water trailed down the stall wall, two fat tears trailed down her cheeks.

Elsa scrubbed for half an hour until all signs of the graffiti were gone. It had taken her mind off the hunger, but now she was worried about how she would make it through the afternoon. Stomach growls would have been quenched if she had eaten lunch. She needed to find something to eat, to stave off suspicion.

The lunchroom was clearing of its last few stragglers. Elsa walked slowly, not looking anywhere directly, instead trying to see everything she could with her peripheral vision. She sat down near an abandoned tray with an unfinished plate of fries and pretended to rummage through her backpack. No one seemed to be paying attention. She folded the paper plate and shoved it into her pack and zipped it up only halfway.

She carried the tray nonchalantly to the stacks by the garbage. A few boys passed by her, dropping their refuse on top of the teeming garbage on their way out. Elsa couldn't help but notice the last boy's paper bag seemed to land with a thud. The round crumpled shape on the top of the heap beckoned to her, hinting at a store of uneaten delights within.

With one last scan of the room, she circled close to the garbage, pretending to throw something in. Using the tray to block anyone's view, she snatched the paper bag and slipped it into the top of her backpack and then stacked the tray in one slick move. She darted quickly out of the room with a surge of excitement.

After days of just bread and eggs, the carrot sticks, apple, and a yogurt tasted like heaven. The cold greasy fries did not, but she wolfed those down anyway to fill her stomach. Washing her hands, she looked at herself in the mirror and felt a burst of pride. Another problem solved...for now, at least.

The afternoon seemed to take forever to pass. Luckily, the final period was an assembly. The class shuffled out of the classroom to line up outside the auditorium.

While they were waiting, Breagh swooped up from behind her and reached into the back of Elsa's collar to inspect the tag.

"I knew it!"

Elsa flinched and batted away her hand. "Don't!"

"I thought I recognized that shirt. It was one of my rejects," gloated Breagh to Lenore and Gabby.

Elsa could feel her face becoming red again. Not because her thrift store shirt had Breagh Brooke's nametag ironed under the tag. It was much, much worse than that.

When she had jumped away from Breagh, Elsa had accidentally passed gas. It was one of those recognizably noxious ones that slip out silently, but you know will create a cloud of nauseating stench within a few seconds. Days of eating nothing but eggs followed by a feast of healthy fiber had taken their toll. It was only a matter of time before everyone would smell it, and she was stuck in this stupid line!

Lenore was the first. Her jaw dropped and her body writhed away, with her hand over her face.

"Oh. My. *Ggggg*!"

The other two girls burst away next, covering their noses. It was so gross, they could hardly even laugh or ridicule. Other kids on either side began to grimace and move away.

Breagh, Lenore, and Gabby held on to each other and began to erupt with laughter at last.

"That is just wrong," Breagh blurted out, in between hysterical gasps. Lenore and Gabby squealed, turning into rubber. They could barely stand.

Might as well make this work in my favour.

Elsa stood taller and stared straight at Breagh with the same blank stare that she knew intimidated Ms. Witherspoon.

All three of the girls froze for a second. Then Elsa gave the slightest shrug.

"You should stay away from me."

Her dark brown eyes bore into the bullies, stupefying them. At last the line really began to move into the auditorium and the mean girls flowed away with the river of students.

CHAPTER 3

Elsa yanked away the piece of plywood. Her heart leapt to see her precious blue bag had not been discovered. She calculated the safest route to the bottle exchange in her mind and hustled to make it there before it closed.

Cutting through the old graveyard, she made good time.

Caw! Caw. The crows announced her presence from various trees above.

Rrrrrllll. A crow swooped over her and something shiny dropped ahead. Elsa put down her bag and sifted through the grass to find it. Her cold hands clasped something hard and turned it over. It was an old gold brooch with an opal stone.

A crow fluttered and settled in a tree beyond her.

I could kiss you, crow!

"*Crrlllll!*" Elsa called up to it, her heart dancing with gratitude at her luck. The crow seemed to spread its wings a bit as it found its perch. She could have sworn she saw missing feathers in the right wing.

Now she formulated a whole new plan. She stashed her gleaning bag in a bush at the back of the graveyard and changed course, heading straight for the pawnshop.

"Aren't you Dana Doran's kid?" asked the red-faced old man behind the counter as he fingered the brooch with suspicion.

Elsa opted to stay silent and leaned in, looking at the brooch. The man's whiskery chin lowered to show a blackened and yellowed pointy-toothed smile.

"Yep, you're hers, all right." His eyes narrowed. "Did you steal this?"

"No."

"Well, where'd it come from then? 'Cuz you and I both know that if Dana had her mitts on this she'd have been in here with it long ago."

"She doesn't know about it. My grandmother gave it to me," Elsa lied.

The man burst into a wheezy laugh that transitioned into a raspy cough. "Yes, well, she's quite the piece of work herself!" His wiry shoulders shook and his breath stank of tobacco as he pushed one steady stream of air out as silent laughter.

Are you going to give me money or not?

Elsa lips tightened as the man finished enjoying his own supposed joke.

"Forty bucks."

"What? It's gold!"

"Dipped. Take it or leave it, pussycat."

Elsa knew there was no negotiating. This man was an expert in smelling other people's desperation.

"Fine," she blurted through her gritted teeth.

She palmed those bills off the counter and headed straight for the grocery store.

A hot chicken, a block of cheese, some fruit, whole-wheat bread, oatmeal, peanut butter, milk, and cookies came to thirty bucks and change. She knew the cookies and chicken were a bit of a splurge, but she deserved them.

The house was dim and still on her return. No shoes by the door, but she checked the bedroom just in case. Empty.

Before putting away the groceries, Elsa hid the remainder of her money under the loose insole of her sneaker. The sun set as she feasted on the still-warm chicken and peanut-butter toast.

Caw. Caw. Caw! Caw!

A continuous stream of hundreds of crows flew over her backyard like a highway, all heading in one direction, for their roost in the park. In the distance, she could hear them gathering in the trees by the thousands, calling the wayward stragglers home.

Ding! The doorbell startled her. Then dread set in. Who would it be? How would she deal with them?

She studied the shadow through the window. It was her Aunt Claire.

"Hi!" Elsa bleated as she opened the door, hoping cheeriness would mask the emptiness of the house.

"Hi." Claire smiled, too, but her eyes darted around the room, looking for clues. "Everything all right? I've been calling your mom for days with no answer."

The phone lay on the coffee table, long abandoned by her mom due to lack of minutes.

"Oh yeah. The battery stopped working for some reason. She's trying to decide whether to repair it or just get a new one," Elsa lied again.

Claire moved into the kitchen. She opened the fridge and seemed surprised and impressed to see all the food in there.

"Where's Dana?"

"She took the bus up to the mall to look at phones." Elsa's lies were getting good.

Claire seemed convinced by the logic. Her face looked pale, with dark circles under her eyes.

Turn the tables. A sense of plenty makes the home front seem calm.

"Do you want something to eat?" asked Elsa.

Now Claire looked a bit ashamed. "No, I'm fine. Thanks. I've got to get back to the store. Keep me in the loop, okay? I get nervous when I don't hear from you guys for a while."

"Sure." Elsa followed her to the door. Claire paused awkwardly, looking at Elsa.

Elsa couldn't hold her gaze. Claire reached out and gave her arm an awkward little rub.

"Tell your mum I came by, okay?"

"I will."

"Take care."

Elsa closed the door and turned the bolt, letting out a big sigh of relief. But then, of course, a bit of sadness set in.

There had been many times Elsa had wished she had been born Claire's daughter instead of Dana's. Claire was cool and artistic. She ran her own shop, selling homemade jewelry and art, and it always seemed like a treasure trove of awesomeness whenever Elsa visited.

Elsa looked up to how Claire had found a way to make her weirdness work for her. Her aunt had grown up with the same troubled childhood as Dana, but had come out of it a rock, instead of the crumbling ball of sand that Dana could be.

Elsa tidied up the kitchen and did her homework. With all the stresses of the day behind her she realized she was exhausted. She took a shower and was in bed before 7:00 p.m.

At 2:00 a.m. she awoke at the loud crash downstairs.

"Whoopsies! Sorry, Elsa!" her mother shouted cheerily.

Elsa raced downstairs to see her mother raiding the fridge.

"Hello, darling!" She gave Elsa an overly forceful squeeze and then messed the top of her hair with an obnoxious rub. "You seem to be doing fine, Peachy!"

Elsa flattened her hair while Dana rooted around various stash spots, hoping to find something. Elsa followed her around the house.

"Claire came by tonight."

"Uh-huh?" Her mother opened drawers and dumped over jars in her room, to no avail.

Then she barged into Elsa's room and began to do the same. Elsa tried not to look at the sneaker tucked under the bed.

Finally her mother stopped and looked at her. "Do you have any money?"

"No. I need some."

Her mother rolled her eyes as if disappointed in her and zoomed past Elsa. "Yeah, you and me both, honey!" she shouted as she raced down the stairs in her clompy high heels.

By the time Elsa got to the bottom of the stairs, her mother was already heading for the door with the remaining chicken, cookies, and bread in hand.

She didn't even turn back as she said, "Love you!" and clip-clomped into an idling muscle car that was waiting out front.

And just like that, Hurricane Dana zoomed off into the night.

Elsa numbly turned the latch to lock the door. She lay in bed for hours staring at the ceiling.

Caw! Caw! Caw!

At the grey light of dawn, the crows were the first to stir in the city. Elsa decided to get up.

It was still very dim as she made her way down to the park. The weather had warmed overnight, melting the dusting of snow. The bare black trees were filled with the silhouettes of thousands of crows cawing loudly as they swooped up in groups, chasing others out, then settling again.

Caw! Caw! Caw! Caw!

The sound was deafening as she joined them in the stand of trees. It surged as they reacted to her presence and flapped up into the sky, flitted around her, then settled again. She closed her eyes. It felt good to be immersed in their chaos.

But she had a lot to do before school.

Elsa returned home and cut cheese cubes and made peanut-butter cracker sandwiches. She packed them neatly and tucked her homework into the backpack. A waft of greasy fry oil poofed out.

Laundry. It has to happen.

She couldn't wear the striped shirt again, but she pulled on the lavender pants and a T-shirt she had hung outside to air out the night before. She gathered up her clothes and a few towels and stuffed them into a shopping bag.

Elsa counted the money in her shoe. $9.36. If she dropped off her clothes at the laundromat, she could go grab her stash of bottles and cans and cash them in at the exchange during the wash cycle. Then, if she hurried back, she'd still have enough time to get the clothes in the dryer before school started. Would it be safe to leave clean, dry clothes there all day? She decided to risk it.

Once she had purchased the overpriced little box of soap and started the washer, Elsa was down to $4.36.

"I'll be back in a bit," she said to the woman folding clothes in a trancelike state behind the counter.

Elsa glanced at the clock. It was 8:15. She had to hurry.

The bag was wet with dew when she pulled it out of the bush. She shook it off and jogged along the quickest side streets to the bottle exchange.

Luckily there was no line when she got there. But the two guys who took in the cans were in no hurry. They casually unloaded her bag and slowly sorted the items as they joked with each other.

Come on!

"There's $5.15 for you, dearie," said one at last. "Don't spend it all on candy, now."

"Thanks," said Elsa flatly. She had no time for jokes.

She sprinted back to the laundromat and loaded $4 into the dryer.

"I can't get back for these until after school. If I gave you a dollar, could you take them out and set them aside for me?"

The woman gave a forlorn smile. "Don't you worry, honey, I'll take care of 'em."

Elsa gladly kept her buck and bolted for school. At about a block away she heard the second bell ring.

She slid into the classroom out of breath. Ms. Witherspoon looked at the clock and looked back at Elsa with disdain as she took her seat. She unzipped her backpack and smoothed out her crumpled homework. It smelled like fries.

Despite her full belly, Elsa had a hard time concentrating all morning. It was hard to care about what had happened in ancient civilizations when it took everything she had just to make it through a day. Ms. Witherspoon could feel her distraction and kept asking her pointed questions.

At last it was recess. Elsa took the doodle she had been working on outside with her. Leaning up against the wall, she disappeared into her sketch of a crow with wings outstretched.

Lenore, Gabby, and Breagh paraded by in their matching brand-named fleece sweaters.

"Artsy *fartsy*," Breagh stressed over-loudly as they passed.

The other girls snickered.

Elsa pretended not to hear it, but inside her blood boiled.

Why do people who have it so easy make it so hard for everyone else?

"Nice purse!" Lenore shouted at Eh Ta Taw, the Karen boy. He carried a traditional hand-woven cotton bag over his shoulder every day.

Eh Ta Taw didn't flinch. Instead, he surprised them by piping up in a very clear and mature voice: "I am proud of my Karen heritage."

"Ka-ren? Isn't that a girl's name?" scoffed Gabby.

"Goes with the purse," hissed Breagh.

The girls scuttled away haughtily, but Elsa could see they were thrown off guard by his strength. She felt ashamed of their teasing him after all he had been through.

"Don't let them get to you," Elsa called out to him.

"Oh, I don't," he said with confidence.

He makes it look easy.

Right after school, Elsa went to pick up her laundry. The woman at the counter lifted up a basket all neatly folded.

Elsa was shocked by the little act of kindness. "Wow, you didn't have to fold it for me."

"It's okay, sweetie. Seemed like your day was a bit crazier than mine."

Elsa tucked the bundle of clothes into her shopping bag.

"That's really nice of you. Thanks."

"Anytime, kiddo."

Elsa thought about treating herself to a ginger ale, but decided she had better hold off and see how things went for another day. About a block away from her house, she stopped to tuck her remaining money back in her shoe.

As she opened the door, she saw Claire sitting at the table looking worried and haggard.

"What's wrong?" asked Elsa.

"It's your mum."

The hospital waiting room was hot and stuffy. Claire had said very little, so Elsa knew it was bad. She had seen two cops talking to a stern-looking nurse. Doors swung open and closed. Nurses zipped to and fro with furrowed brows and busy feet. No one was around to answer any questions. The chairs were uncomfortable.

Claire broke the long silence. "Are you hungry?"

Elsa shook her head, tight-lipped. "When are they going to tell us something?"

Claire gave a helpless shrug, rubbing her forehead.

Elsa was going to burst with frustration. She had to do something. "I can get you a tea if you want."

Claire looked up. Her eyes were loving, but wistful. "Elsa, that would be wonderful. Thank you." She fumbled through her leather bag and handed Elsa a bill. "Get yourself whatever you want. I'll have a peppermint with no milk."

Elsa wandered through the long hallways. The stale air, bright lights, pastel walls, and bad art seemed to push in at her from all sides. She felt like a wild animal being forced into a pen. A scream was welling up inside her.

She started to run. She ran past the café. She ran out the front doors. She kept running. She ran into the stand of woods behind the hospital. The scream erupted.

She sank down onto the ground and burst into tears.

After a few minutes, they stopped flowing, but her guts continued to spasm silently. There was a surreal peace as a warm wind tossed the leaves around her. She almost felt as if she was under the sea.

"Hullo," a startlingly close voice called out above her.

She looked up with sudden alarm. There was no one there except a crow on a branch in a tree nearby.

"Hullo," it said again.

Elsa couldn't help but giggle. "Oh. It's just you." The crow adjusted its perch on the branch and looked at her expectantly. "Hello," she said. The crow seemed satisfied with that and flew off. She brushed the leaves off her butt with a little smile.

Elsa had heard of people keeping baby crows as pets. She had always wanted one. Without fail, they flew off eventually, but she had heard stories of crows learning to repeat words and even coming back to visit their former owners.

Logically, Elsa knew that the crow that had said hello must have been raised by a human. And the crow in the backyard, the graveyard, and this tree were all just...chance experiences. There were thousands of crows in this city; each encounter surely must have been with a different crow. But walking back to the hospital, Elsa couldn't help but think about how cool it would be if they had all been the same crow. She delighted in the idea of having a crow looking out for her.

Claire took the tea and change with a quiet "Thanks." She could tell Elsa had been crying, but didn't press it. Elsa was relieved that Claire didn't prod about where she had been.

"They've got her stabilized."

"What does that mean?"

"We should just go home for now. She's going to sleep for a while."

"What happened?"

"There was an incident downtown. The police were called. But, it's all...well, it's over now."

"What *happened?*" Elsa was sick of being treated like a child. "Why won't anybody ever tell me anything?!" she squealed with frustration.

Claire let the echo of the shout settle down the hall. She looked into Elsa's burning eyes. "All right. I'll tell you in the car."

The world was grey and wet as they drove.

"Dana was pretty revved up. She was raving and singing on a rooftop."

"Why is that such a big deal?"

Claire sighed as she changed lanes. "She was naked."

Elsa was stunned.

If the mean girls find this out, I will never hear the end of it.

"Anyways, she was making a scene. The cops were called. She wouldn't go easily. She threatened to jump."

"What?"

"I don't think she had that intention when she went up. I think she just added that to the drama when they tried to bring her down. But it complicates things now. There will be a mandatory observation period at the hospital to make sure."

They pulled up to the house. Elsa and Claire sat still in the car, the heaviness of the truth sinking in.

"How long were you on your own, Elsa?" asked Claire after a while.

"Five days," she mumbled softly. She tensed, waiting for the scolding.

"Wow," said Claire quietly. "You did a really good job."

Surprised not to be in trouble, Elsa floated into the house.

Claire was definitely the coolest aunt ever.

"But you know you can call me anytime, right?"

Claire closed the door behind them. The house seemed neat and tidy. Claire inspected the forlorn cupboards and fridge.

"I guess I'll go get some Chinese. I have to grab some work from the store anyway. I have a big order to finish."

Elsa nodded, slumping into a kitchen chair.

"Are you okay?" asked Claire. "I promise I won't be long."

"Just don't take five days," she said dryly. Claire couldn't help but crack a smile.

Alone in the house again, Elsa took the money out of her shoe and put it in a jar on the windowsill. Outside, the light was fading and the highway of crows flew over the house, heading for the park. She listened to the beckoning calls.

She slipped on her coat and out the door. It was unusually mild for a late November evening. The air filled her lungs and relaxed her shoulders. She followed the trail of crows to the park.

CAW! CAW! CAW! CAW! CAW! CAW! CAW! CAW! CAW! CAW! CAW! CAW! CAW!

The sound of their calls was deafening as she entered the dim woods. They streamed in from all directions as the sun set, settling in the bare branches. There were so many crows it was as if the trees had leaves again, made of black.

A crow swooped down and flew low, straight towards her. She stood still, hoping it would fly close. As it glided nearer, she saw two gaps in the right wing. Her heart lurched with excitement, then a pang of sudden fear. The crow was flying directly at her!

She froze her body and her fear. Elsa could feel the wind on her face as the crow's wings gathered above her and it landed right on top of her head.

Its body was surprisingly light and its talons surprisingly gentle as it perched in her hair. It looked down at her from above.

"Hullo." The crow tenderly studied the shape of her head with its feet.

"Um, hello," she managed to croak, looking up with disbelief.

"Oh, don't mind me. The rest of the crows seem to think they might need a new queen, so I was just testing your head for crown suitability."

"What?" Elsa couldn't help but laugh. The crow lurched up in the air to accommodate the sudden movement of her head and then settled right back down. The weight of his feet even felt kind of nice as he pawed at her scalp.

"Yes. Suitable, very suitable."

Elsa laughed again, but this time he held on. He peered down at her from his perch.

"Actually, I was really just hoping to see if I could make you laugh."

"It's hard not to when you're having a conversation with a crow on your head," beamed Elsa.

"Good. Well then, I have done my job, whether the queen is here or not."

"Your job?"

"I'm Cracks. The jester." He lifted one foot up off her head and held it in the air, waiting expectantly.

Not sure what to do, she held up one finger towards his foot. He clutched it firmly and gave her finger a little shake.

"Very nice to formally make your acquaintance."

"Uh, it's very nice to meet you, too. I'm Elsa."

CAW! CAW! CAW! CAW! CAW! CAW! CAW! CAW! CAW! CAW! CAW! CAW! CAW!

There was a burst of volume in the symphony of crow calls. With a flurry of flaps they erupted out of the trees and into the air, sweeping in all directions.

"Oh, please do excuse the other crows. They've got their feathers all in a ruffle."

"How come?" asked Elsa.

"Normally the queen chooses the trees we will roost in for the night and now they are arguing about High Crow and Low Crow."

"What does that mean?" wondered Elsa.

"Well, certainly not what *they* think."

Elsa's eyes were getting tired from rolling up to look at him. Cracks seemed to sense it. With a gentle pump of his wings he was up and then down on the ground below her.

"So sorry. Is that better?"

"Uh, yes, thank you, Cracks."

The crows flitted above from tree to tree, unable to settle. The light was almost gone.

"It's almost dark, Elsa. I should go up. You had better get back, too."

"Okay," she mumbled. She didn't really want this to end.

"I'll see you again," Cracks said, as if reading her mind again. He disappeared into the flurry of black.

"Goodbye," she said to the chaos in the woods.

When Elsa opened the door, she saw, for the first time, Claire making the customary "grown-up" scowl.

"Where were you?" she demanded.

Elsa could see that beyond the anger, Claire had been beside herself with worry.

"I went for a walk in the park."

"Why didn't you leave me a note?"

"I'm sorry. I didn't think. I guess I'm just used to having run of the roost."

The crows quieted in the distance.

Claire released a big sigh and started serving out the Chinese food. Elsa set the table with plates and took her place. She noticed a little tremor in Claire's hands as she doled out the food.

"I didn't know what to do. The last thing in the world I want to do is call the cops about you right now, okay?"

Elsa slurped her noodles. She understood what Claire was implying. Social workers would probably be checking in as it was.

"It won't happen again," Elsa promised soberly.

Claire softened. Her sad, loving eyes gazed deeply into Elsa's as if seeing into her very soul. Not used to such attention, Elsa went back to focusing on her plate.

"I'm not mad. I'm just stressed out," said Claire in a tired voice.

Elsa nodded and enjoyed the warm, yummy meal in silence. A restaurant meal was a rare treat, but even more than that, Elsa was glad to have company at last.

As they cleaned up together, Claire handed Elsa her mother's cell phone.

"I put some minutes on this," Claire smiled with a knowing wink.

CHAPTER 4

Caw! Caw!

Elsa awoke with the crows. She found Claire asleep on the couch with her jewelry pliers still in her hand. Elsa gently pried them from her grasp and covered her up with a blanket.

Quietly Elsa ate breakfast and packed a lunch of leftovers. Claire didn't stir. Knowing she must have stayed up late working, Elsa didn't want to disturb her just to say she was leaving, so she left a note:

Went to school. Thanks for everything you do. E

She thought about signing it *Love, E.,* but chickened out.

Elsa had not stopped thinking about Cracks since their encounter. She made sure she had enough time to take a detour through the park on the way to school.

She listened to the caws and followed them into the woods. She came to a clearing in the middle of the woods near Dead Man's Pond. With a large throne-shaped stone by the pond and trees all around, it seemed like the perfect place for crows to hold court. She found the crows flying to and fro in state of confusion.

"Make way! Make way! Make way for the princess!" shouted a swooping crow in a shrill voice.

"Yes, make way! The princess is waiting!" added another anxiously, swooping back and forth over the pond amongst a mess of other crows doing the same.

No one was listening. Crows took perches on tree branches, then picked up and flew around again in a great tizzy. It was as if no one knew what to do or where to sit.

The largest crow in the whole group landed beside the stone and jumped up and down, flapping his strong wings. "EVERYONE TAKE YOUR PLACE!" he bellowed in a deep, commanding tone.

Still no one paid attention.

"Huzzah!" yelped Cracks, as he did an awkward double somersault in the air and landed directly in the seat of the stone throne. He spread his sparse wings wide and shouted, "I hereby apply for the job!"

The shock of seeing the jester where the queen should have stood had a settling effect on the chaos. Everyone quieted down and took a spot to listen. Cracks saw Elsa spying in the woods beyond and gave her a private wink with a glint in his eye. Then he bowed graciously to the group.

"Just kidding! I'm sure someone else can do a much better job." Cracks gave a sidelong glance to Lustre, a shiny black crow who stood with a regal air just off to the side of the big crow.

"Ahem, yes," said Lustre, narrowing his eyes at Cracks and then shooting a darting look of disdain to the big crow, Boughbend.

Boughbend shrank a little, but then puffed up his chest as he jumped over behind Lustre.

Lustre stepped in front of the stone and turned to address the group with charm. "Now that I have all of your attention, if it would please the court, I humbly request to welcome the princess to stand on the throne, while the queen is…while the queen is…" His noble manner diminished slightly as he paused as if at a loss for words.

"Where is the queen?" "Where is she?" "Where is the queen?!" suddenly burst out hundreds of shouts from the masses of crows in the treetops.

It was total cacophony.

Lustre was very uncomfortable now. He motioned to the princess, hoping she could calm them down.

The princess circled down from her perch and alit on the stone throne, followed quickly by her two shrill-voiced ladies-in-waiting, Breezy and Careen.

"Be quiet for the princess!" screeched Breezy.

"Listen to the princess!" wailed Careen.

"BE QUIET!" shouted Boughbend.

"Ahem!!" screamed the princess herself.

"What's happened to the queen?" "Where is she?" "Is she hurt?!!" continued the waves of shouts from the treetops.

Cracks took it upon himself to fly up above the throne and then dive-bomb straight down into Dead Man's Pond with a loud splash.

It stupefied the crows into an attentive silence. He came out, his whole body wriggling with shivers. He flapped to shake off the water and warm up. "Well, she's not in there."

Elsa smiled.

He's helping them get what they need and they don't even notice.

With quiet restored, the princess turned back to Lustre. "Yes, so where is she, Lustre?"

Lustre cringed. He loved nothing more than being minister of the court. The power, the prestige, the position in society. The only thing he would have loved more would be to be a king himself. But he had not been named for that.

"The queen is...the queen is..." He paused, looking around at all those wanting eyes. All those wanting eyes that he loved to captivate, but who wanted an answer he did not have. Their silent, expectant gaze was unbearable.

"The queen is *indisposed* at the moment," he blurted out at last, trying to sound as official as possible.

The princess looked at Breezy and Careen. They shrugged and shook their heads with confusion. The princess looked back at Lustre.

"Indisposed? What does that mean?" she whined.

"*Indisposed*?" "Indisposed?" "What's indisposed?" "Has someone gotten rid of her?" "Where is she?!!" came hundreds of whispers and shouts from the crows in the trees.

This time Lustre didn't care if they shut up or not. And he certainly wasn't going to beg them to quiet down. He glared up at them with a look of superiority and they soon settled, waiting for an answer.

"Indisposed means she is unavailable at the moment and we must wait patiently for her return."

Elsa noticed Cracks smile a deep smile of satisfaction to himself.

"But why?" "Why?" "Why?" "Why?" "Why?" cawed the masses of crows all around.

Lustre chose not to answer that question and instead parted his wings and bowed deeply to the princess to signal that the court was over. She gave a small curtsy and lifted off, followed by her ladies-in-waiting.

As was customary, the crows dispersed to seek out their day's food and entertainment on their own or in small groups.

Lustre flew away quickly, to avoid direct questioning from the princess, but also hoping he'd be able to find the queen first if he searched.

Or better yet, he thought, *maybe I'll find her dead.*

Lustre's eyes narrowed as he realized that what he had first seen as an embarrassment might end up being an opportunity. He soared as high as he could.

Cracks and Elsa were soon the only ones remaining in the clearing. Cracks waved his straggly wing. "Ahoy, Elsa!"

Elsa waved back and approached her new friend. "You seemed to be very happy with what Lustre said about the queen," she said, hoping he'd tell her more.

"Yes, indeed," smiled Cracks. "He got the right answer, even though he has no clue where she is." He giggled with a look of impish delight. "Plus, I most thoroughly enjoy watching Lustre squirm."

"Do you know where she is?" Elsa asked.

"The queen of the crows?" asked Cracks.

"Yes," said Elsa, smiling. "Who else would I be talking about?"

"I don't know," said Cracks flatly.

"Oh," sighed Elsa, a little disappointed, since she was all wrapped up in the mystery now.

"But if you are talking about the queen, well, she's gone to the Hollowing Tree, of course."

Jesters.

"The Hollowing Tree? What's that?"

"I'd tell you all about it, but you've got to go get in in your cage now."

"My cage?" asked Elsa, perplexed. Then it dawned on her and she smiled. "Oh! You mean school."

"School? Is that how they teach your young folk? How can anyone learn the ways of the land in a box?!" Now it was Cracks who was perplexed.

"Yes, I've often wondered that myself. They let me out for fresh air three times a day. Come visit me!"

"Aye," said Cracks, drifting off into thought. "I will if I can, Love."

Elsa nodded softly. She realized he had bigger things on his mind.

It was time for her to go to school and face another day. She scampered off through the woods with her mind full of thoughts of crow court, the Hollowing Tree, and this mysterious queen. She also couldn't help but savour the way he had called her "Love."

CHAPTER 5

Elsa squeaked in just in time, denying Ms. Witherspoon the opportunity to scowl at her. Her homework was complete and she knew all the answers when asked. But she was completely bored and all morning drifted in her mind to the world of the crows. This seemed to make Ms. Witherspoon even more disgruntled.

The lunch bell couldn't come soon enough. When at last it did ring, she grabbed her lunch and headed straight outside. Her restaurant Chinese lunch would have gained her some points in the lunchroom, but she didn't care.

It was cold, so very few other children dotted the schoolyard. She munched her noodles, scanning the trees and field for Cracks.

Caw! Caw!

There were a few crows here and there, but no sign of her friend.

Her knuckles felt tight bracing against the wind. She slurped up the last of her lunch and went in to warm up in the library.

She sat down at a computer to search information about crows. At the computer next to her, Eh Ta Taw sat very straight, with his traditional Karen handwoven bag draped over his shoulder, reading something very seriously. She studied the curves of his nose and cheeks, his stern brow. She could tell he would grow up to be very handsome.

Instead of looking up crow behaviour, she typed "Karen

People" into the search. She read about Burma, also called Myanmar, a small country in Asia where a strong military and monarchy had ruled for decades over the people, denying them good healthcare, education, and many other freedoms. The Karen people, a northern tribe in the country, had actively resisted this oppression for years as soldiers in a civil war, insisting that they wanted to be their own country.

Elsa scrolled through horrific pictures of people with their legs, arms, and eyes missing from stepping on land mines. These were explosives that the government had buried along the borders of the Karen-held territory that would explode if stepped on. She read about hundreds of thousands of refugees, some who had to walk through land-mined areas, hoping to seek refuge in neighbouring Thailand. Karen children were being born into refugee camps and growing up there, unable to leave the camps and never knowing their own country. But despite the hardships, the Karen people refused to give up their struggle and continued to wage war from both sides of the border.

He has been through so much! No wonder the schoolyard antics don't make him flinch.

She sighed and paused at a disturbing photo of a coffin set on top of many logs and several burning tires. It belonged to Saw Than Htoo, a famous Karen rebel leader. This was his funeral pyre after he was assassinated by Burmese forces.

"That was my uncle," said Eh Ta Taw, making Elsa jump. He tapped gently on the photo on the screen. "He was a great general."

Elsa swallowed uncomfortably. She wanted to say so much, but felt paralyzed.

"He gave me this bag," said Eh Ta Taw stoically, sitting a little taller.

"You have a lot to be proud of," she mumbled softly.

He gave a slight, firm little nod. His dark, full eyes went back to his screen. Elsa closed down her computer. Crows seemed like child's play after reading all that.

As the clock slowly ticked away the afternoon, Elsa felt more and more like she was in a cage. She shifted in her seat uncomfortably. Monsieur Gopaul droned on about conjugating verbs in French. She felt that feeling of bursting at the seams again. She tried to breathe and crunch the feeling down, but felt her arm shooting up uncontrollably.

"May I go to the washroom?" erupted loudly out of her mouth.

Monsieur Gopaul's shoulder's slumped at the chalkboard. He didn't even turn around.

Lenore and Gabby snickered quietly and looked at Breagh. Breagh knowingly mouthed the word *diarrhoea* and all three of them swallowed their giggles.

"En Français, s'ils vous plaît, Elsa." He continued writing out his verb tenses.

"Les toilettes, s'ils vous plaît, Monsieur Gopaul," she muttered.

Without looking back, he gave a dismissive flick of his chalky hand.

Elsa looked over at the mean girls. The eager look in their eyes and gaping smiles tipped her off that something was up.

Elsa stared straight into Gabby. She enjoyed watching Gabby shrink in her skin a bit. Then Elsa very deliberately grabbed her best graffiti pen and shoved it in her pocket. At least now she was armed.

She felt the pressure of the cage release a bit as she burst into the hallway. She didn't really have to go, but she figured she could kill some time in the bathroom and try to repress the scream that was building up inside her.

As she walked to the washroom, rage flickered inside her like a flame.

Why do I even have to ask an adult permission to use the toilet? I have been taking care of myself for years and you need to tell me when I can pee?!

The cool, stale, damp air of the washroom had a calming effect. She ran her hands under the tap and splashed her face. This line of thinking wasn't helping any. She cleared her mind and ran her wet hands through her thick hair to dry them. She puffed out a big sigh at her reflection in the mirror.

Now onto this mean girl business.

Elsa opened each stall down the row. In the last one, in the same spot where she had found the comment about her mom, was a poorly drawn cartoon of her with a poof of cloud blowing out her behind. Above, it said: *Elsa drops fart bombs!*

Elsa spent the next ten minutes drawing a pretty good rendition of Breagh's head under the fart cloud. For good measure she added Lenore and Gabby standing behind, looking horrified.

As much as she wanted to stay in the cool stillness of the bathroom, she knew she could only milk this little escape for so long. One advantage of being an eleven-year-old girl was that teachers started to give you more graces with bathroom time. She didn't have her period yet, but they couldn't be sure, and she had noticed she could push these bathroom breaks a little longer with no questions asked.

She slipped silently back into the class. Monsieur Gopaul droned on, writing out French onto the chalkboard that no one was paying attention to.

Breagh, Gabby, and Lenore looked at her with blank faces but then sheepishly grinned to each other.

Obvious little schoolgirls.

Elsa burrowed her head into her book, fastidiously copying the verbs onto the page.

At last the end-of-day school bell rung.

As she left the schoolyard, Eh Ta Taw walked just ahead of her, by himself. Elsa thought about catching up to walk with him a while, but she opted for the park instead.

Lustre had flown high all day. As one of the highest crows in High Crow society, he prided himself on his ability to look down at everything from above. Also, it had conveniently kept the Low Crows from pestering him for answers about the queen. He had circled the entire city from the highest heights for hours and had even ventured far into the outskirts but had seen nothing. He realized he was famished.

From his high vantage he spied a young female crow who had just pulled a choice-looking pizza crust from a garbage bin. He spiralled down to grab it from her. She squawked as his talons pierced her foot. He snatched the crust from her clutches and soared up to a high tree to feast.

After wolfing down the crust, Lustre swiped her blood off his talon with his beak and savoured the taste. He was in the mood for something more than pizza.

Lustre lifted up high above the trees and houses to scan the vicinity. There were no other crows in the area. The little injured crow hobbled on the ground below, one foot curled up in great pain. He tilted down and dropped out of the sky, soaring at full speed for her tiny neck. With a quick squeeze she went silently limp and fell over sideways. Lustre took a quick look around to make sure no other crow had seen, and with two swift pecks he ate out her eyes.

"Oh, I am so tired," yawned the princess. "We simply can't have another roost like last night's."

"That was terrible," Breezy agreed. "I hardly slept a wink with everyone flitting about, not knowing where to land or when to quiet down."

"Everyone should know a black crow doesn't fly at night," scolded the princess.

"Yes, but the Low Crows need the High Crows to keep them flying *straight*," sniffed Careen. "What will we do if the queen hasn't returned? Who will choose the roosting trees?"

Breezy and Careen looked cautiously at the princess, who was preening her feathers absentmindedly.

"Well, I certainly hope *someone* does, because I simply can't have another night without my beauty sleep," said the princess, not picking up on their hint.

Breezy and Careen shared a quiet, helpless look. Though they knew it wasn't their place to say, both felt it only natural that the princess should take up the queen's responsibilities in the queen's absence. It seemed this hadn't even occurred to the princess.

"Do you think she could have gone to the Hollowing Tree?" wondered Breezy.

The princess sat up abruptly from her preening. "Now? But why would she go there now?"

"Perhaps she's considering your name?" Careen placed the question delicately, hoping to plant the idea of queenliness in the princess's mind.

Breezy and Careen shared a look again.

The princess shifted uncomfortably side to side on her branch. "My name! But I am too young to be queen! And she's a perfectly wonderful queen. Why would she want to pass it on to me now?"

Breezy and Careen had to admit all that was true. But in their hearts they couldn't help but feel a little disappointed that the princess wasn't showing any signs of leadership in their time of need.

"It must be some other matter," soothed Breezy.

"I'm sure she'll be back as soon as she can," cooed Careen.

The princess's ruffled feathers settled as she went back to preening.

Boughbend couldn't fly quite as high as Lustre, but he had spent the entire day circling the city as high as he could. He too had ventured far out into the outskirts, but had returned with no news. As the protector, Boughbend felt positively sick not knowing the whereabouts of his queen.

Why didn't she tell me? he wondered. He was very hungry, but he couldn't bring himself to take a break. He lifted up into an updraft and began to circle again.

Boughbend loved his queen more than anything he could think of. Her soft, strong voice; her kind, luminous eyes; her sharp mind. As protector, he was privy to almost her every interaction, and he held her in the highest regard because he had never once seen her make a selfish decision. Without fail, her choices were always fair, sound, and what was best for the individual or group, even if it meant more trouble for her. Boughbend knew that it was the queen who was the true protector of the group. He only hoped he could become more like her, the more he served her.

As Boughbend meandered over the same circles he had traced all day, his mind began to drift. The hunger and the repetitive gliding were making him feel spacey. Suddenly, his body clenched as he saw two young foxes fighting over something black below. He pulled his wings back tight and tipped his broad, sharp beak towards the road to drop out of the sky at lightning speed.

It was definitely a crow they were fighting over. It seemed too small to be the queen, but he had to find out.

"*CRRRRRrrrrrrrrrrrllllllllkkkkk,*" he hissed as he swooped and pecked at the two foxes on his first pass.

One fox let go of the crow to bite back at him. He turned

tight on his wing to circle back quickly as the other young fox tried to make a break with the prize. With one strong draw of his powerful wings, he extended his talons for her face. She ducked and dropped the carcass and both foxes scuttled off sheepishly.

Boughbend settled close to the body. Even though it wasn't the queen, his heart still sank. It was Berry, the little daughter of Ruffle and Popcan.

He felt anger well up in him from his very core as he examined her wounds. He could see where the foxes' teeth had dug into her wings as they tugged. But they had not killed her; they had found her dead. He could see the clench of talons in her neck and her two eyes pecked out. This was most definitely the work of a bird.

"*KRRRK, KRRRKKKKK, KARRRRRRRK*!" He sounded the alarm.

A few trees down, a crow repeated it. Another crow repeated it even farther down the block. He heard the alarm call spreading out in all directions throughout the city in the distance. He gently picked up Berry and carried her back to the park.

Much to Lustre's chagrin, most of the other crows were already gathering around the clearing by the time he arrived. He had been far out in the outskirts when the alarm had reached him, calling him back. He assumed the queen had returned and he wanted to be there to greet her and give a sense that all was under control in her absence. Of course, a small part of him couldn't help but hope that she had been found dead.

His stomach tightened when he saw Berry's body lying delicately before the empty stone throne. Boughbend stood over her, at solemn attention. The princess was nearby with her head buried in the wings of her ladies-in-waiting. Cracks stood with his head bowed, far off to the side. Lustre spiralled down and took his place close to the throne.

"One of ours!" "One of ours!" "It's one of ours!" the crows cawed loudly from the trees around the pond.

More and more crows streamed in from all directions, including Ruffle and Popcan.

"Nooooooo!" screamed Ruffle as she swooped down and landed sobbing over her daughter's tiny form. Popcan huddled close, spreading his wings over her and the body. "*Caaaaaaaaaaaw, caaaaaaaaw*," they moaned with grief.

Out of respect, all the crows in the trees fell silent and bounced back a branch or two. Boughbend and the others all stepped back two steps. Lustre held his place.

"What happened? What has happened to my Berry?" demanded Popcan, enraged.

"I found her being fought over by two city fox pups," said Boughbend respectfully.

"But you can see by her wounds this is clearly the work of birds," announced Lustre commandingly to the group.

"The gulls!" "The gulls!" "It was the gulls!" erupted the masses in the trees. Their howls were deafening.

Cracks cast a sidelong glance at Lustre and saw a flicker of smile dance through his dull, cold eyes.

Use their fear to control them, thought Lustre.

Gulls' feet are webbed; they can't squeeze around a neck like that, thought Boughbend.

"Boughbend!" shouted Lustre. Boughbend stiffened, standing taller.

"Fly close to the princess!" Lustre commanded.

That goes without saying, thought Boughbend, with a surge of anger.

"Everyone else, get ready to take your formation for the procession! We fly undaunted!" Lustre turned to Ruffle and Popcan and bowed graciously. "We await your signal."

"*Caa-aaaaa-aaaaw,*" sobbed the parents quietly. They bent over her body for a few minutes while the rest of the crows held silent. After a while, they looked at each other and nodded. Tenderly they gathered each wing in their grasp and lifted Berry's limp body up into the air.

They flew her up over the trees and headed for the river. With a deafening roar of caws, the entire group of crows lifted up, forming a circle of protection around them as they made their way towards the shoreline, the domain of the gulls.

Arr! Arr! Arr! alarmed a group of gulls as the crows flew over en masse.

Several crows darted down to threaten, as the rest of the group flew out over the water. Other crows dropped feces as they passed.

Boughbend, on high alert, took in information at all levels. The locations of the gulls, the shape of the group, the position of the parents, the tears in the princess's eyes.

Cracks hung respectfully at the back of the group. He knew that no one wanted to see the jester on an occasion as sombre as this.

Lustre flew high above everyone, to remind them that he could. Gradually, he let the group get ahead of him and then quietly he turned wing, slipping back to the park unseen.

Soon Ruffle and Popcan slowed, way out over where the river met the sea. Satisfied they were far enough from the gulls, they let Berry's body drop into the river. Thousands of crows flew in circles above, blackening a section of sky, shouting: "One of ours!" "One of ours!" "Berry was ours!" "She was one of ours!"

Ruffle and Popcan flew wildly, careening and speeding to release their grief. Surrounded by their tribe, the parents wailed out their sorrow, while the rest of the group hovered over the body, waiting for it to sink.

Disinterested in emotional affairs, Lustre had slipped away to take advantage of a moment alone with the throne. He spiralled down and touched the firmness of the stone with great satisfaction. He had always wanted to know what it felt like to stand here. Alone in the clearing, he savoured the feeling and admired how the sun reflected off the sheen of his shiny black outstretched wings.

A twig snapped behind him. He instinctively flapped out of the throne and then laughed at himself. It was only the red-headed girl. He stepped deliciously back onto the stone as he watched her make her way closer through the woods.

He had seen her many times. In fact, he had often thought that she seemed somewhat crowlike. She seemed to be a part of her people, yet separate. Just as the crows were a part of the city, but ignored. Plus, she was fond of digging through the garbage and collecting shiny things.

She paused as she approached the clearing and saw him standing on the stone.

"Are you the queen?" she asked in a friendly tone.

He leaped off the throne with a shot of nerves. *How does she know about the queen?* He shook his ruffled feathers back into place, trying to regain his composure.

"Where is everyone?" she asked, peering up at the empty trees.

Will she understand me if I respond? I had better not. Lustre tilted his head and pretended to be just another stupid crow, as he usually did with humans.

She stepped closer to examine him. "Oh, you must be Lustre. Are you allowed to stand on the throne while the queen is gone?"

Lustre felt a bit of urine slip out as he took flight in a panic.

How does she know me? he wondered, completely mystified. *Is she the queen's spy?*

He flew out of her sights as quickly as he could. Panting on a branch, he watched her search the woods a little longer, then make her way back towards the houses.

Perhaps I have underestimated the power of the queen, he thought.

Walking home, Elsa thought it was odd not to see the usual stream of crows trailing back to their roost by this time in the evening. It was bad enough that the queen was missing. She certainly didn't want them all to disappear!

She expected to see Claire when she opened the door, perhaps looking a bit disappointed because Elsa hadn't texted to say she wouldn't be coming straight home from school. Instead the house was still and dim.

Elsa felt a little pang of sadness not to see Claire there. She liked the idea of coming home every day to her steady, calm energy. She climbed the stairs and checked to see if Claire was napping in her mother's bedroom. The room was tidied, with the bed made neatly. Without signs of her mother's chaos, Elsa felt another pang of sadness.

She had been trying not to think about her, but now she couldn't help but wonder what was happening in the hospital. Claire had said that because her mother had threatened to jump off the roof they had to keep her for three days for "observation," whatever that meant.

Elsa climbed onto the bed and buried her face in the pillows. She could smell the faintest trace of her mother's hair. She turned over and stared blankly at the ceiling for a long time in the quiet, darkening room.

In the distance, at last she heard the crows and she felt the tightness in her stomach relax as their caws drew nearer. She allowed two tiny tears to drip down the sides of her cheeks.

The sky streaked pink and orange as the group made their return with the sinking sun. Thousands of piercing caws echoed across the water and resounded through the park. Humans walking their dogs along the boardwalk stopped and pointed at the massive morphing black shape that travelled ever closer. The gulls lay low and gave them no guff as they passed over the rock embankment. The group returned to the clearing to find Lustre standing in front of the throne. He opened his wings wide.

"Ruffle. Popcan. Our hearts and song are ever with you."

The mourning parents softly tilted their heads.

"It has been a difficult day for us all and there will be much to discuss tomorrow. But for now we have an urgent matter to address," said Lustre in a grave voice.

He relished how they all leaned in, hearts almost pounding now, hanging on his every word. "We need a peaceful sleep tonight. If it would please the court, might I humbly suggest that the princess select our roosting trees tonight?"

Breezy breathed out a sigh of relief. Careen stood taller, relishing the idea.

"Me?" squealed the princess. "But how should I know?"

Lustre's eyes narrowed with satisfaction. *She has taught her nothing.*

"It is of no matter," said Lustre quickly and authoritatively. "I am happy to oblige if the princess so desires."

"Yes. I so desire."

Careen sank. She knew she would have been the one to really make the decision if the princess hadn't so easily passed her power off to Lustre.

"She so desires!" "Lustre will choose!" "Follow Lustre!" And other such caws rippled through the trees.

And with that, Lustre felt like a king. He lifted up high above the park and studied their options. Thousands of crows followed him up, flitting through the dimming sky, waiting for his signal. He had no idea what the queen looked for when she selected which trees they would roost in for the night and he didn't care. He was going to enjoy faking it to the fullest degree.

He decided on the stand of trees between the baseball diamond and the large open field, and banked sideways towards them. The whole group followed suit, shouting: "It's Lustre's choice!" "Lustre has chosen!" "Follow Lustre!"

Elsa clumped down the stairs and meandered into the kitchen. She saw a note from Claire saying she might be late, but that there were groceries in the fridge.

She opened the door and saw a sight she had never seen. The refrigerator was absolutely packed with food! Juice. Jam. Little yogurts for lunches...it was like a box from heaven had arrived.

Most kids have to be pressured to eat their vegetables, but not Elsa. Her eyes almost popped out of her skull when she pulled open the drawer and saw red peppers, broccoli, carrots, onions, and more. Living with her mum had meant a lot of white bread and eggs and she was sick of it. She eagerly pulled the veggies out onto the counter and started chopping.

It was after seven when Claire burst through the door.

"I'm sorry I'm so late," she called out, unloading a bunch of tools and craft supplies onto the floor. "Christmas shoppers! It's a love/hate relationship."

Claire looked up and saw the table set for two. Elsa stood

at the stove, putting the finishing touches on a veggie stirfry.

"Elsa, it smells amazing in here!"

Elsa gave a shy little smile. Claire came to take to a closer look at her creation.

"Who's taking care of who here, huh?" Claire asked with a smile, tousling Elsa's hair lovingly.

Elsa shied away a bit, not accustomed to such attention. But when she turned back, hoping for more, Claire was already grabbing the plates.

"You are an absolute dream," said Claire with her back to her. Elsa felt a warm glow wriggle through her body.

They served out the meal and sat down at the table. Claire was obviously starving. She wolfed down a big bite.

"Mmm," she said, chomping her mouthful, "dee-licious."

They ate in the happy silence that comes when hungry people are enjoying a good meal. Occasionally Elsa looked up, stealing glances at her wonderful aunt ploughing through the food.

Elsa felt a layer of tension releasing from her body. Maybe her cells were celebrating the return of much-needed vitamins and minerals. Or maybe, for the first time in a long time, she just felt happy.

"Thanks for getting groceries," said Elsa when they were done.

Claire looked at Elsa with that wistful gaze again. "Of course, honey."

"I know you are really busy. I can do the shopping and laundry and stuff," offered Elsa.

Claire gave a pursed little smile that seemed like she would refuse, but then she just said, "Thank you." A bit of tension released from her shoulders, too. "It's going to be a bit crazy for a while. I am behind in my orders and I can't get anything done at the store with Christmas coming up."

Elsa looked at the pile of work by the door. "Why don't you get started? I can do the dishes."

Claire sank back in her chair and stared straight into Elsa. Her eyes welled up with a glistening sheen. Unaccustomed to all this direct eye contact, Elsa felt awkward. She quickly picked up the dishes and took them to the sink.

"No matter what Dana may have said to you in the past, I want you to know that you are a wonderful kid, Elsa."

Elsa felt that glow ripple through her body again, but as much as she wanted to look up and smile into that spotlight of love, it was somehow too much to bear. Instead she filled the sink and gave an awkward little nod.

"Young woman, really," added Claire.

Elsa felt another layer of tension begin to melt. It felt so good to be recognized for how well she had held it together for the past week. Past *years*. As Dana's younger sister, Claire had a good idea of how crazy and hard it had been.

Elsa also liked how Claire wasn't prying her for details. There was an unspoken respect and understanding that flowed between them. Like soldiers who had come through the same war.

After the dishes were done, Elsa joined Claire in the living room. Tools, wires, and various bits of weird, cool-looking stuff were strewn all over the coffee table. Claire was hunched over a little sculpture of a robot built out of old watch parts and circuits. Claire's work always had a distinctive steampunk look. She had a way of seeing beauty in things that other people threw away.

"Cool!" said Elsa.

"It's a new line I'm working on," she said through gritted teeth that held a tiny screw. "And it's selling like hotcakes," she added with a tone that almost sounded like regret.

Claire worked the tiny screw into place and then looked up. "Want to come hang out at the shop tomorrow?"

"Yes!" squealed Elsa with the unmistakable exuberance of an eleven-year-old girl.

When Elsa awoke, the sun was high. It was the latest she had slept in for a long time. She stretched her arms out like wings. The clock said 9:44 a.m.

Downstairs, she found Claire asleep with her pliers in her hand again. Six beautiful little robot sculptures sat on wooden bases covered in cylindrical glass domes on the coffee table. Elsa was pretty sure the shop opened at ten.

She went into the kitchen and packed a bag of apples, yogurts, granola bars, and the leftover stirfry.

Elsa had noticed that Claire had brought a glass pitcher with a mesh plunger and coffee with her when she'd moved in. Elsa put on the kettle and pulled up the plunger to clean out the old coffee grounds that sat at the bottom of the glass contraption.

Once it was clean, she tried to pour about the same amount of grounds in. Noticing the kettle was about to boil, she quickly flipped the lid so the whistle wouldn't wake Claire. She wanted her to have every minute of sleep she could afford.

Elsa carefully poured the boiled water over the grounds and set the little mesh plunger on top. She paused for a second, wondering how long she should wait before she pushed the plunger down. The grounds and water swirled into a brown soup. She decided to go for it. Slowly and carefully she pushed the mesh down, which collected the coffee grounds and pushed them down to the bottom, leaving a clear, dark rich drink above. Proud of herself for figuring it out, Elsa decided it was time to wake Claire.

"Claire, it's ten to ten," said Elsa softly, holding a travel mug full of coffee by her nose.

Claire startled awake with a jump and a look of horror. When she saw the packed bag and coffee in front of her, she relaxed back into the couch for an instant, rubbing her eyes.

"Oh my goodness, Elsa. You are a life-saver."

They packed everything up into the car quickly and scooted to the shop. Claire turned the sign from closed to open at 10:01.

Elsa absolutely loved Claire's shop. It was like nothing else in their small city. Electric blue butterflies encased in glass, skulls of little animals, large drippy beeswax candles, and, of course, the original works of art that Claire created made it seem like you had stepped into a futuristic antique otherworld. Elsa felt a swell of pride at how Claire had made her weirdness work for her, instead of feeling like a freak that didn't quite fit into society.

Even better than the shop was the mess behind the counter. Boxes and bags of odds and ends lined the workbench. Bits of watch gears, little bronze octopuses, metallic buttons, chains, fabric, and feathers were strewn everywhere. It was a treasure trove of cool things to discover.

On the other side of the workbench was a small cot. Claire had lived at the house with Dana and Gran when Elsa was born. But she moved out when Elsa was about three to go to art school. Now she lived at her store.

Elsa looked around at all the amazing raw materials as Claire set out the new glass-domed robots on the counter.

"You can make something if you want," she offered.

"Really?" exclaimed Elsa.

"Of course," she said with a grin, sipping her coffee and looking up to welcome the first customers of the day.

Elsa sifted through a pile of pre-made metallic shapes. Skulls, hearts, hands, keys, starfish, flames... There was so much to choose from!

Claire put on interesting music that Elsa enjoyed much more than the radio her mother normally played. Customers came and went. When they went, Claire dug into half-finished projects, answered phone calls, and researched supply orders online. Elsa studied the hunched line of her high shoulders and could see where the dark circles under her eyes came from.

"How you doin' over there?" asked Claire. "Bored?"

"Not in the least!" squealed Elsa.

She had sifted for hours through piles of raw materials and had decided on a few pieces she wanted to attach into a necklace. A heart, two wings, and a crown.

"Can I attach different pieces of these together?" she asked.

"If you want to learn how to use a soldering iron you can," said Claire with a twinkle in her eye.

"Really? You'll teach me?" Elsa couldn't believe Claire would let her use the hot metal-bonding tool.

"Of course," Claire nodded. "It's not that hard, you just have to be careful."

Claire showed Elsa how to make the little dabs of molten metal that acted like glue between the metallic parts. Elsa attached the wings to either side of the heart and then the crown above it.

"I really like your design," said Claire. "It's a classic."

Elsa held the piece up to admire her handiwork. "I was hoping to make it into a necklace."

"Bonding the loops for the chain is a bit trickier. How 'bout I do that part?"

Elsa nodded with a smile and handed her creation to Claire. The phone rang. Claire set the piece down on the counter and answered.

"Hello?"

Claire listened for a while. She let a big sigh out as she closed her eyes and pinched between her eyebrows. Her shoulders seemed to draw up closer to her ears.

"Yes, I understand. I can be there in ten minutes."

"What's wrong?" asked Elsa. "Is it Mum?"

"No," said Claire. With another sigh, she wrote a note that said *Gone For Lunch* on a piece of paper. "It's Gran," she said flatly.

"I can stay and watch the store if you want," offered Elsa, trying to be of help. She knew that Gran could be as big a handful as Dana sometimes.

"Knowing you, you probably could. But it's Saturday. And you're a kid! Go to the park or something. I won't be more than an hour." Claire taped the paper onto the door and turned the sign back to CLOSED.

Elsa grabbed a yogurt, apple, and granola bar for herself and then handed Claire the bag as they locked up the store. "Here. You might as well actually have lunch while you're gone."

Claire smiled and took the bag appreciatively. "Thank goodness someone's got their act together in this family!"

Elsa squirmed, but enjoyed the sidelong compliment. Claire waved and sped off in her car.

Walking along the riverside road that led to the park, Elsa met Cracks in the old oak trees that lined the promenade. From a low extending branch he spread his straggly uneven wings to say hello.

"Cracks! I've missed you," beamed Elsa.

"Odd, 'cuz I'm awfully hard to miss." He spread his gapped wings again, for emphasis, then smiled, shifting his weight side to side on the branch.

"I came looking for you yesterday, but all the crows were gone, even though it was sunset."

"Aye, 'twas a very sad day yesterday."

Elsa paused, wondering if he would elucidate, but he just seemed to drift off.

"I thought I had found the queen, but it was just Lustre standing on the throne."

This broke Cracks out of his drift. "Lustre was standing on the throne?"

"Yes," said Elsa.

"While all the crows were gone?"

"Yes," she nodded again.

"Hmm. Interesting. Very interesting." His eyes narrowed and he seemed to slip off into a drift of thought again.

Elsa felt as if she would burst with curiosity, but she also wanted to respect his space. He seemed to be pondering something of great importance.

"I hope I didn't get Lustre in trouble," she said after a while.

"Trouble?" exclaimed Cracks, returning from his reverie. "Oh, don't ye worry about that, dearie. He's doing a plenty fine job of that himself, i'n't he?"

Elsa shrugged with an uncomfortable smile. It was all a bit confusing.

Cracks seemed to be reading her mind again. He relaxed and gave her a comforting smile. Then he tilted his head and peered closely at her.

"You've done excellently, Elsa." And after a pause, "The queen did say ye had an important role to play."

"The queen? The queen knows about me?" queried Elsa.

"Well, of course she does!" cackled Cracks as if it was common knowledge. He looked down at her wide-eyed face and cackled again from the depths of his guts. For some reason he found her shock quite hilarious.

"But why would she know about me?" Elsa asked again quietly, completely mystified.

"Well, because…" Cracks tried to contain his laughter. "Because…because…" And then he burst into hysterics again.

Elsa was trying to get a serious answer, but the longer this went on the more she found herself finding it funny as well.

"Because why?" She smiled despite herself.

"Well, because," Cracks managed to blurt out between laughs, but he gasped so desperately for air now, it became contagious and Elsa found herself giggling.

"Because…?" smiled Elsa.

"Because," peeped Cracks with great difficulty as his body bobbed up and down, trying to repress the laugh.

But the peep sounded so ridiculous that Elsa couldn't help but really laugh now. And that burst Cracks's true laugh out fully and he laughed so hard he rolled back and fell out of the tree.

That sent the two of them into another, even fuller, round of hysterics. For several minutes, each rolled around in the grass trying to stop laughing, but every time they looked at each other it would start another gale of laughter.

After much quaking, they regained control of their bodies.

"What were we talking 'bout, then?" asked Cracks at last.

Elsa snorted one more time at the ridiculousness of it all.

"I forget," said Elsa.

Now it was Cracks who snorted. Realizing that she had just heard a crow snort sent Elsa into another fit of laughter. Her face and ribs were hurting now, but the rest of her felt giddy.

Gradually, the surges of silliness began to dissipate and at last they lay quietly staring up at the sky. A crow flew high overhead.

"The queen knows about you because any High Crow worth their feathers knows about *you*," said Cracks softly.

Elsa inhaled this thought, not knowing quite what to make of it.

Cracks rolled onto his back and used the momentum to jump back up on his feet. "Do you have any snacks?"

Elsa sat up and rummaged through her coat pockets. She pulled out the yogurt and apple. Cracks tilted his head disappointedly. She found the granola bar in the other pocket.

"Ahh, that's more like it." He hopped a few steps closer.

Elsa opened the package and gave him half. She snacked on her lunch, staring at the river, wondering what it all meant, as Cracks pecked away at the piece of granola bar.

"Will you tell me more about the Hollowing Tree?" she asked.

"Aye, I can," said Cracks with a satisfied little smile. It was as if he had been waiting for her to ask. "Follow me."

Cracks picked up and flew ahead across the field. Elsa followed him into the paths that led through the woods.

"The Hollowing Tree is the place of sanctuary for the leader of the crows," explained Cracks as he hopped along the dry, leaf-littered path. "It's the place they can go when they need a break from the group to seek perspective. And, of course, it's where they go when it's time to find the name for the next in line."

"Why didn't she just tell someone where she was going?" asked Elsa.

"Aye, it's a good question, isn't it?"

They passed the crows' court at Dead Man's Pond and went farther on up the hill and into the next clearing in the woods. It was a crossroads. At the nexus of paths stood a great old Ash tree with wide-spreading, thick branches and a huge, knobbly, knotted thick trunk.

"Is that why you haven't told the others where she is?"

Cracks gave a self-satisfied little smile and swiped one side of his beak with his wing tip. She waited for him to say something, but he just hopped onward towards the tree.

Of course Elsa knew this tree. She had passed it many times on her walks through the park. But she realized as she approached that she had never really stopped to take a good look at it. Above its massive trunk opened up a deep hollow in the centre of the tree. She placed her hand on one of the bumpy gnarls and leaned her head in and looked around inside the great opening. Other than a few leaves, sticks, and old candy wrappers, it was empty.

"Is this it?" she asked.

Cracks blinked knowingly, with the slightest nod.

"But where is she?"

Cracks gave a mischievous grin. "It's quite the conundrum, i'n't it?" he said wryly.

"Oh, Cracks. Is this all just a jest?" Elsa wondered.

Cracks's eyes twinkled as he jumped up onto a low branch. "Anyone can put their head into the hollow of a tree, but ye can only enter the Hollowing Tree if ye know the queen's name."

"What's her name?" asked Elsa innocently.

Crack leaned in and whispered very seriously, "Only the High Crows can know."

"Oh," said Elsa, a little disappointed. "I understand."

"No, I don't think you do," giggled Cracks.

Elsa smiled and shook her head. Hanging out with a jester was fun, but it led you around in circles sometimes.

"No, I guess I don't."

"No matter." He flapped his wings. "Your auntie's probably a-worryin' by now."

The cell phone in her pocket rang. Cracks flew off as she fished for it in her coat pocket.

"Hello?"

"Hey, it's me. I'm back. Where are you?"

Elsa searched the trees around for Cracks, but he was gone.

"Just here at the park. I won't be long."

"All right. I'll put the loops on for you and then you can choose a chain."

"Okay," said Elsa.

"You okay?" asked Claire. "You sound sad."

"No, I'm great." Elsa tried to perk up. "How's Gran?"

"Oh, you know..." said Claire with resignation in her voice. "Gran is Gran."

"Okay, well, I'll see you in a bit then."

"'Kay, bye." Claire hung up.

Elsa took one more look inside the tree hollow and tried to think of a queenly crow name.

"Silken," she whispered. "Onyx," she tried again. "Winter-sun. Moonlight." The breeze picked up and whistled through the hollow.

It was no use. It was like trying to guess someone's password.

"They miss you," she whispered into the tree, and then she turned back onto the path.

On her way back through the field, she came across a crow trying to peck the crust of a sandwich out of a sealed plastic tub. The crow was so caught up in trying to liberate its prize it didn't even notice her approach. Pecking down at the ground and voraciously at the tub, the crow seemed almost reptilian, reminding Elsa that birds are the descendants of dinosaurs.

She realized there were several other crows spread out around the field doing basically the same thing. Their eyes and beaks were aimed down, their intent on just what might be on the ground in front of them.

Above her a few crows could be seen ambling through the sky, using the power of the wind to fuel their flight.

They must see so much from up there.

Elsa had always wanted to be able to fly. She once had a dream where she hovered and soared about a metre above a beautiful, calm, blue sea. Her mother had been there, too, and they had flown together, holding hands over a pod of leaping dolphins. It was the best dream she had ever had.

As Elsa walked back along the promenade, she watched a high-flying crow scanning over the river. Just in front of her another crow picked at the ground, barely moving away before she was within a short pace of it.

High Crow and Low Crow.

It seemed interesting to Elsa how different the approaches to seeking nourishment were—thinking only of yourself and the small prize at your feet, or taking in the vast vantage of the whole community and all its intertwining relationships while getting your needs met at the same time.

"Well, well, well," she heard from the tree above.

"Oh, hi, Cracks," she beamed.

"What else did you notice?" he asked.

Elsa wasn't sure what he meant. He looked the same as before. "About the tree?" she wondered.

"No, about the crows."

Could he really be reading my mind?

"Um, well, that flying high to seek food seems safer. I nearly stepped on that crow back there."

"Aye," he said with sparkling eyes, as if he was proud of her. And then he flew off again.

The shop was busy when Elsa returned. Claire answered people's questions and helped get art pieces off the wall. Elsa was happy to see her doing a good business, but she could tell Claire was tired. Even though Claire put on a friendly face for the customers, Elsa knew she would have rather been hiding in the back making something with her hands. Or maybe just flat on the cot.

Elsa noticed the uneaten stirfry leftovers still in the bag behind the counter. She took them out and started warming them on a little hot plate behind the cot.

She is so busy taking care of everything else she forgets to take care of herself.

Elsa served out a few bites for herself and then left the rest for Claire. While chewing she fingered the beautiful winged and crowned heart they had crafted together. She sifted through the chains to find one that matched the piece.

When Elsa had started the necklace, she thought she would give it to her mom. But now that it was complete, she found herself wanting to give it to Claire. She felt a pang of guilt about that.

She decided on a thin, square-shaped silver chain. It was delicate, but strong. Like Claire. She laced the chain through the loops and held it up to admire the full effect.

"Beautiful and strong," said Claire behind her, "just like you."

Before she knew it, Claire had snatched the necklace from her and clasped it around Elsa's neck. Claire circled around to see how it sat.

"Fit for a queen," she said with a smile.

Was it terrible to wish that her mom would never get out of the hospital?

Elsa swallowed that thought. She smiled at Claire and looked down at her chest. She decided to keep it over her own heart for a while, to decide.

"Thank you," beamed Elsa, venturing to give Claire a full gaze of love.

Now it was Claire who flinched, as if it was a bit too intense. She looked away quickly, spooning up a big bite of veggies.

"No, thank *you*," Claire said through a mouthful. "Listen, I'm going to be here for hours. You can go do something fun if you want. I've got to take these downtimes to churn out this big order."

"I could help," offered Elsa.

"As useful as your little fingers would be, I refuse to become a sweatshop!" said Claire jokingly. "No, seriously, don't you want to call a friend or something?"

Elsa's face dropped instantaneously. Despite her immediately trying to mask it, Claire could see that Elsa didn't have a friend to call.

"Or the library!" she blurted, trying to make up for her blunder. Claire obviously felt terrible. She fished on the desk and grabbed a twenty-dollar bill. "You could go to the mall?"

"No, that's okay," said Elsa, refusing the money. "I'm happy to go back to the park. I'll just meet you at home."

"Okay," said Claire, looking deflated.

Boughbend circled over the outskirts for the third time.

"Boughbend, I'm getting tired!" whined the princess puffing behind him, trailed by Breezy and Careen.

He had realized he had made a grave error leaving the princess's side yesterday to go searching. Today, he had convinced her to come with him.

"Don't you want to find your mother?" He pressed onward.

The princess reared up her wings. "Well, of course I do! But I don't want to kill myself doing it, do I?" She circled down to the nearest tree and put her feet down with a pout. Breezy and Careen sheepishly joined her by her side.

Boughbend flapped one hard pull to vent his frustration, then turned wing to join them. She had him by the feathers.

She panted as she adjusted her perch. "I'm positively starving."

Boughbend remembered he hadn't eaten for days. It was a passing thought. He looked at Breezy and Careen. "Go find her something."

The girls picked up and flew over to a nearby cornfield. Boughbend looked at the princess and felt remorse.

"I'm sorry," he said quietly.

She preened herself quietly, still pouting.

Boughbend fidgeted on the branch. Words were never his strong suit. And he knew his quick temper was his weakness. The queen had reminded him many times that being protector meant protecting hearts, too, not just bodies.

"Of course you want to find your mother. You want to find her just as much as I do. I am grateful you've joined me in the search."

"Do you think she's gone to the Hollowing Tree?" the princess asked, staring off at the cornfield.

"She never has before. Your mother is a tireless queen," he said, speaking from experience.

"Was she worried about anything?"

"Not that I am aware of," said Boughbend contemplating.

She surely wouldn't be going to get the princess a name yet. She's not ready. She may never be, he thought to himself.

Breezy and Careen returned with a big, old, dry ear of corn.

"There's a bunch more, fallen on the ground by that old

barrel," reported Careen, handing the corn to the princess.

"Okay, you stay here. I'll go get some more," said Bough-bend, taking flight. "And stay up!" he shouted back. "There are coyote in these parts."

Lustre had mobilized the group to search the outskirts. He feigned that this was a good way to avoid gulls as well. In truth, he wanted to be alone with the Hollowing Tree.

He hopped onto the lip of the hollow. Nothing happened. He ventured inside. Still nothing. It was an unassuming, splintery old stump. He hopped back, half-glad that nothing had happened. It would have been a great sacrilege to disturb the queen on her sojourn if he had been taken through.

"Doesn't feel as good as the throne, does it?" said a sarcastic voice.

Lustre jumped. His eyes narrowed at Cracks. "Why aren't you on the outskirts with the search?" he demanded, angry at himself for being startled by the lowest of the Low Crows.

Cracks ignored the question, preening his messy, misshapen wing. It was a lost cause, but he carried on very regally, as if he were the princess.

"You never should have set perch on the throne," said Lustre, looking down his beak with disdain.

Cracks guffawed. "Oh, don't worry, *I* know my place around here." He flapped up and away.

Lustre's eyes narrowed as he watched him fly on.

I don't like his tone, he thought. Then a little knot of worry began to creep into his stomach. *Could Cracks have spoken to that Low Crow red-headed girl?*

Lustre had no idea when or even if the queen would return. How would he deal with things if the girl was, indeed, a spy? Cracks, he could handle. The queen would certainly take his word over that filthy mess. But this mysterious girl was a thorn in his side.

Whenever Lustre felt uneasy, he was comforted by visiting his secret stash. He flew there now.

He kept his treasures in the broken top of a high street lamp, surrounded by a branchy oak tree in the middle of town. House keys, earrings, screws, bottle caps, coins, a toy car. He was quite sure his collection of shiny things was the finest of all the crows'. Except of course the queen's.

His heart leapt! The queen's treasure was unguarded with all the crows away on the search mission. Dare he push his luck so far? He couldn't help but fly back that way, while he contemplated his strategy.

Essentially, he had to play two games simultaneously. Hide behind the princess's weaknesses and control her, while stirring up fear in the group to make them want to give him power. But the tricky part, and this was what was troubling him, was making sure that nothing he did would put him in bad favour if the queen did return suddenly.

He arrived at the circular stand of birch trees in the middle of the park woods where the queen's treasures were kept. No crows were about, but a flock of gulls flew over.

The queen couldn't possibly have gull spies, could she?

Lustre could hardly believe that she would. Gulls were lower than even the lowest crow.

She wouldn't trust them as far as one flap, would she?

Now he was filled with doubt. The girl's and Cracks's statements had thrown him. He did not like this feeling. He was accustomed to using fear, not being consumed by it.

Still, generations of crow tribute lay all around him unguarded.

He was aware of the things various crows had brought to this queen during her tenure, but imagine the treasures that might be in those hollows, collected by the generations of crows that came before!

She might not even know.

It would stand to reason. This queen was certainly gracious when gifts were brought to her, but Lustre knew her heart didn't burn the way his did when she looked upon the precious glint. He remembered the look she gave him last spring when his heart went wild with desire after Popcan had brought her that beautiful butter knife. It was as if she could feel the emanations from the burn he felt inside.

"Remember, Lustre, it's just a thing. True shine comes from within," she had said with a look of reproach.

Plus, she spent ever so much time dealing with the crows and their problems, she probably hadn't even bothered to do a thorough inventory of the entire cache of shiny things.

Now desire burned through his fear and made him bold.

This opportunity will never come again.

With the gulls long passed and no crow on the horizon, Lustre sprung into action. He quickly examined the hollows, from birch to birch. Anytime he saw any modern house keys he passed on. At last he found a hollow with keys of a different shape altogether. The nails were built differently as well. Even the jewelry seemed heavier and of better construction.

He grasped onto the lip of the hollow with one foot and flapped his wings as quietly as he could to stay up. Quickly, he darted his eyes side to side, seeing no bird. He thrust his claw into the hollow and grabbed what he could. As he took flight, he transferred the haul into both claws. This shiny was heavier than he expected. As he awkwardly tried to adjust the weight, he dropped a key. He watched it fall into a deep pile of leaf litter with a thud.

Arr! Arr! Arr! sounded a group of gulls fighting over some food on the road ahead.

Lustre squeezed his claws tighter and pulled them in tight to his body to hide the shiny. He looked back, but couldn't see the key.

No matter, I'll search for it later.

He leaned into the wind to shield his feet from the sights of the gulls below. Lustre flew as fast as he could to his street lamp across town to examine his booty.

Elsa crossed through the large field. Gulls peppered the park, but there wasn't a crow in sight, which was odd. With the thousands of crows that roosted in the park, she couldn't think of a time when she'd walked through the city and not seen a crow or heard a caw. But there was an odd silence today.

They must be searching the countryside.

Arr! Arr! Arr! A gaggle of gulls passed over.

It wasn't really a silence, Elsa realized. It was the fact

that the crow music was missing from the symphony of city sounds.

Elsa watched some other gulls pester each other as she crossed the road to the tennis courts. She thought about how they were just as much a part of the park as the crows were, yet she hadn't observed them closely. They hadn't captivated her in the same way as the crows, so she had ignored them.

I wonder if they have kings and queens?

Elsa decided to start paying more attention to the ways of the gulls. She also decided to start paying more attention to what she paid attention to.

The concept of taking in a High Crow version of the world tantalized her mind.

As she entered the wood, she practiced expanding her perception. Instead of just looking at the way in front of her, she softened her vision to take in the broadest vantage she could, including all her peripheral vision. She listened. She felt the wind on her skin. She smelled the mud, pine, and dry leaves mixing together.

There was so much going on.

Even with her gaze looking forward, she could still see a big brown dog bounding through the woods far to her right. Its owner followed slowly, walking with a slight limp of his right leg. In the distance to her left, a mother pushed a baby carriage, crunching leaves along a path. Behind Elsa, tennis balls bounced and a father coached his boy on his swing.

All around, the city was rich with layers of sounds, ranging from the hum of a cruise ship, loud trucks rattling down the promenade, and children playing on the playground beyond the wood to a distant pinging of city construction downtown.

Thoonk. Elsa's foot knocked something under the leaves along the path.

She stopped and rooted through the leaves to find what it was. Brushing the leaves aside, she found a small, old-fashioned key.

She examined it more closely. It had been made by hand in a forge. It looked to be a hundred years old.

Elsa picked it up and put it in her pocket. How interesting that practicing High Crow perception had yielded treasure right below her feet. This new way of seeing the world intrigued her even more. She continued practicing all the way home.

Lustre checked over his shoulder as he landed on his street-light. The oak tree that surrounded the lamp clung to some of its leaves over winter, but still he felt exposed. He loosened his grip and let his treasures fall into the cracked-open casing of the light.

At first he was disappointed. The things were so old, they had been tarnished by time and weren't even shiny anymore. A greenish coin. A blackened locket, with faint hand-drawn portraits of a woman and a boy. But then he saw it: a deep gold ring with a sparkling red stone. It was the most beautiful shiny he had ever seen.

He tenderly inserted one of his toes into the ring and rubbed at it with the back of his wing. It became shinier. He worked fastidiously for several minutes, periodically lifting it up to admire how the light bounced off the facets of the stone. He had been polishing for a while when he realized he was hearing caws returning from the distance.

The key!

He dropped the ring into the top of the lamp and shuffled the other treasures over it. He pushed off hard and raced to the park.

When he arrived he could hear the group consolidating and advancing from all directions. Ignoring the gulls nearby he swooped down onto the path where the key had fallen. Frantically he hopped and pecked through the curled dry brown leaves. Nothing.

He flew up and circled over hoping to see a glint, but he remembered the key had been darkened by time. That worked to his advantage. It wouldn't interest a crow if they saw it.

Perhaps a human found it.

The crow silhouettes drew nearer now and he could hear their calls. "To the roost." "To the roost!" "Gather!" "Darkness is coming!"

He landed once more and scratched through the leaves until the crows' calls were almost at the edges of the park. Giving up, he lifted majestically up into their view and flew higher than them all. He circled a few times and chose the stand of trees nearest the water, next to the playground. It was his least favourite place to sleep due to the sea wind that came up the river, but it was far from the stand of birch trees and he liked it for that reason tonight.

Plus, it will make them think about the gulls.

He took the highest tree in the stand and watched as

the group began to amass for their roost in the branches below him.

Elsa reached under her bed for her treasure box.

She had learned the hard way that if she really wanted to keep something in this house, it had to be well-hidden. She had seen her birthday camera disappear. The gold hoop earrings from when she got her ears pierced, the expensive sneakers that "Gran" had given her last Christmas. (She knew they were really bought by Claire, to make sure there was more than just her gift at Christmas.) And, of course, all the money she'd saved from her lemonade stands.

At the height of the upswings, just before her mother was about to crash, she'd usually buy a bunch of stuff that they couldn't afford and Elsa would get presents. But time and time again, after the crash had passed, Elsa would come home to find those belongings had vaporized, along with her mother.

Now anything she really wanted to keep was in a little box she kept taped under her bed. Funnily enough, the things she treasured probably wouldn't have had any value to Dana anyway. Those items had long been sold. Nevertheless, Elsa kept the things that mattered to her hidden, just in case.

She had a silk Japanese doll her mother had bought for her when she was six. The pocketknife Claire had given her for her eleventh birthday. A ribbon she'd won at the science fair. Beach glass and a moonsnail shell from the time Dana had taken her to the beach. A picture of Dana smiling a pure, true smile, holding Elsa as a newborn. And a perfect crow feather she had found in the park.

She added the key to the collection.

She looked down at the beautiful necklace against her chest. She decided to keep it on for now.

Elsa felt relieved when she heard the crows returning. She went to her mother's bedroom for the best view of their air highway to the park. She watched them pass by in the hundreds, cawing loudly, beckoning each other home.

Claire probably wouldn't be back until long after dark. Bathed in the orange glow of the sun, Elsa felt her mother's absence.

She peered into Dana's closet. She took out a frilly leopard-print tank top and a shiny black miniskirt and put them on. She stepped into a pair of gold lamé high heels that were still too big and looked at herself in the mirror.

With the dimming light and the necklace, Elsa looked much older. She wobbled in the shoes over to the dresser and pulled out a pair of socks and a bra. She figured out how to get it on and stuffed the cups with the socks.

She re-examined the outfit in the mirror, turning from side to side, examining her future profile.

What is my future?

Elsa pushed down that thought quickly. Anytime her mind wandered to what was going to happen, she found herself getting knotted up inside.

She kicked the shoes off and put on her own clothes again. She shoved all Dana's stuff back where it came from.

But no matter how she tried to avoid the thought of her future, her mind periodically flickered back to worrying about all the unknowns that lay ahead.

What's happening during this "observation"? What if they deem Dana unfit to take care of me? What if Claire doesn't want to keep me? What will happen then?

It was all too much to bear.

She breathed in the ever-increasing volume of the crow caws. The vibration of their group call to roost calmed her. She needed to get outside.

She went down to the kitchen and stepped out the back door. She held the necklace over her heart. Breathing in the crisp air and listening to the sounds from the park settled her soul. She stepped back in to think about dinner.

Arr! Arr! Arr! A group of gulls laughed amongst themselves as they huddled into the rocks along the shore beside the playground.

Ruffle sank into her branch, listening to them wistfully. "Why has he put us so close to the gulls? I can't stand to hear them laughing," she muttered.

Popcan cuddled up next to her.

"We have to show them we are strong," said Billow from another branch.

"Why do we put up with them at all?" asked Wrapper. "We have numbers. We could push them out of the park if we really wanted to."

"Nobody wants war," said Popcan. "Once it starts, it never ends."

"They may be bigger than us," said Billow, "but we are smarter and can work together. We can't let them think they can take one of ours and get away with it."

"How do we know we are smarter?" asked Whirly. "We only know them from a distance."

"Well, it's obvious, isn't it?" chimed Wrapper. "I detest their pale feathers, ugly feet, and ghastly songs. We should take them out, once and for all."

Boughbend could hear all this from the high tree. So could Lustre. The princess was already sleeping, but Breezy and Careen listened with interest.

Boughbend stole a glance at Lustre. With the night setting in, he couldn't be sure, but he thought he could perceive a subtle smile.

All this talk troubled Boughbend greatly. He knew how hard the queen worked to maintain the uneasy peace between the gulls and crows.

"We all come from an egg and need the wind to fly," squawked Cracks from the lowest branch in the roost.

"Of course he'd say that," whispered Wrapper. "He's no prettier than them."

"Can you believe he had the gall to land on the throne?" gossiped Billow.

"Sacrilege!" harrumphed Wrapper.

"Let's all just get some sleep," said Ruffle wearily.

Careen waited until most of the group was quiet. She relaxed the grip on the hidden treasure she held in her clutches. She knew it might be seen as inappropriate to have collected shiny while she should have been searching for the Queen. But she simply couldn't pass up snatching this keychain when she'd seen it hanging on a nail in a tree.

Best of all, no one had seen her, so she could keep this one for herself instead of feeling obligated to present it to the princess. She took flight to find her hollow.

Over the seasons, she had done her best to find shiny as often as she could to present to the princess and occasionally even the queen. Careen wanted to move up in the ranks and keep favour in her good position. But once in a while, when the rare opportunity presented itself, she hoarded a little stash for herself in a secret hollow in a maple near the tennis courts. She had two coins, a pop tab, and now this fantastic little keychain.

"What are you doing flying in the dark?" barked a gruff voice from behind her.

Careen's heart leapt. It was Lustre.

He had hoped to paw for his lost key a bit while the others slept.

She could certainly be a spy for the queen, he brooded.

"Oh, it's you!" she exclaimed nervously and slowed to settle on the nearest branch she could see.

He followed, landing ominously close. He noticed her awkward, one-footed landing.

"I hope you don't think me terrible." She leaned in a little closer to him, looking up at him longingly.

Now is my chance, she thought as her heart raced. *Don't chicken out.*

She had always admired Lustre's big wings and shiny feathers, but, even more, his powerful position. She had often fantasized about how mating with him would launch her to the best position she could possibly attain. Unless, of course, the queen named her the next queen—but she couldn't foresee that happening.

He never seemed to pay her much attention, though. In fact, over the seasons he had shown no interest in mating with anyone as far as she could see.

"I was..." She lingered uncomfortably, feeling all fluttery inside. "I was...well, to tell you the truth...I was going to hide this."

Careen held the little keychain up to the light from the tennis courts.

"I found it while on the search and I know I should have presented it to the princess, but I really wanted to give it to you." She leaned even closer, extending her foot coyly towards him. "To say thank you for being such a strong leader in our time of need."

She gazed at him as he held the silver loop and pendant up to the light. It flashed and sparkled deliciously as it dangled. She looked away quickly as he looked back at her.

Hmm, he thought. *Does she truly admire me? If she longs for advancement and is willing to break the rules to do it, perhaps she could be useful as my spy.*

"You are very thoughtful, Careen," he said softly. He watched her feathers ruffle up. "Where were you going to put it?"

"Oh." She bowed her head with embarrassment. "I have a little hollow with some other trinkets, just over there."

Lustre handed her back the keychain. "Keep it for me there, with your other things. It will be our little secret," he said, doing his best to sound intrigued.

She giggled girlishly and flew to her hollow and placed it inside. He watched her, taking note of its location, possibly to be raided later.

She returned to him swiftly.

"I have always admired the lean of your wing, Careen. You fly very gracefully."

"Thank you," she said bashfully.

"Have you considered mating in the spring?" he asked directly.

She ruffled, almost losing her perch. She swallowed, trying to regain her composure. Lustre would want a refined mate if he took one.

"Well, I would lose my position as a lady-in-waiting if I did," she said carefully. She paused, extending her neck as regally as she could. She tilted her head away from him slightly, but looked deep into his eyes, with a sidelong glance. "It would need to be worth it to me," she said in a cool, calculated tone.

Lustre felt a strange surge of attraction flicker through his body. He had never even bothered to think about mating before. But it would seem odd if he didn't get on with it eventually. And this one had a thirst for High society. Or so it seemed.

Keeping Careen close shall be useful to me regardless of which side she is on. I will play this carefully.

"Come," he said as tenderly as he could, "let's get you home safe."

Careen straightened with a smile. "Before we return, Lustre..."

Oh, it's so delicious to say his name to his face! She tingled all over. *I must ask now, while I have a chance.*

"Could I fly high with you? I must always stay at the princess's level." She leaned towards him with a hint in her tone. "But I am quite sure I could fly much higher if allowed."

Now it was Lustre who felt his feathers rise. He cleared his throat to regain his composure.

Is she saying what I think she is saying? I would certainly need a mate if I'm to be king.

"I understand how frustrating that can be," he said carefully.

Their eyes locked and an unspoken tingle of conspiracy rushed between them.

"I guess we shall share two secrets, then," Lustre said coldly.

He launched off the branch and volleyed up over an updraft. Careen followed suit. They soared up into the darkness. She had never felt so free.

Lustre watched her as she carefully worked the gusts to her advantage, taking height.

"The wind is stronger up here!" she whispered gleefully.

He nodded, as if to say: *It's true, but don't caw about it.* Careen understood.

They circled ever higher. He had never flown with a female to these heights. She seemed to be navigating just fine.

Wordlessly, he asked with his eyes if she was okay. She blinked back with a smile, gazing up as assurance. They smiled broadly and lofted up another tree's length.

Careen couldn't believe how much she could see. The city lights spread out like an electric spider into the dark web of outskirts. Lustre flew even higher above her. Careen had reached her limit. She admired how effortless he made it look.

If Lustre were to become king, then I could be queenmate, she schemed.

He tipped his beak down towards the roost and they spiralled silently back down to the trees.

The next morning, Elsa awoke late again. She found Claire's thin body sleeping stiffly on the couch. The sprawl of art supplies and empty coffee pitcher on the table in front of her indicated it had been another late night.

Even when she's resting she looks tense.

Elsa decided not to put the kettle on. She wanted Claire to get as much sleep as she could on her day off.

It frustrated Elsa that she couldn't help Claire more. It wasn't fair how much weight Claire carried for this family.

Elsa recognized how deep that tension ran. She knew that Dana had inherited the same mental illness that Gran had and that Claire had grown up in a household where nothing was certain, just like Elsa had.

Elsa had often worried about this generational affliction. She wondered if Claire had ever questioned, as she had, whether she might one day turn out to be crazy, too.

These thoughts were too stressful and Elsa squashed them down.

She grabbed an apple from the bowl and wrote a note that said:

At the park.

She slipped out quietly.

When Elsa entered the woods, she could tell the crows were at court by the caws that rang out from the direction of Dead Man's Pond. She hoped the queen had returned.

Out of respect, she opted to take the path that would allow her to peer at the throne from behind at a distance, amongst a thick grove of closely growing pines. She didn't want her presence to disturb them.

She peeked over the hill. The princess still stood meekly on the throne.

"Berry must be avenged!" shouted Billow from the tree line beyond.

"Hear, hear!" agreed many in the group.

"Why do we put up with the gull menace? This is our park! Those ugly palefeathers should find other shoreline. There is plenty to be had," added Wrapper.

"Palefeathers!" "Palefeathers!" "Out with the lowly pale-feathers!" chanted the masses.

"The queen has always brokered peace with the gulls," piped up Boughbend from his place beside the throne.

The princess listened carefully. "'Tis true."

"But that was *before* they took our Berry," Lustre added quickly with a conniving tone.

"Hmm," said the princess. "That is also true." She tried to sound like she knew what she was doing.

"Take them out!" "Lesser, ugly, savage birds!" "They are lower than low!" "Send them back to the sea!" The jeers became wild and angry in the trees.

Lustre tried to contain his joy.

Boughbend seethed with frustration. "ENOUGH!" he bellowed deeply.

"*Arr! Arr! Arr!*" squawked Cracks from the sidelines, imitating a gull. "Let's get rid of the humans and foxes while we are at it. The queen will be proud of us for declaring war on the whole park in her absence!" He did an awkward somersault and landed on his bum, with his spindly legs spread-eagle.

Boughbend shook his head, impatient with the foolish antics of the jester.

"We have no proof it was a gull at all. Her neck was *crushed*." Boughbend looked up apologetically towards Ruffle and Popcan. "Forgive me," he said to them with respect, and then turned back to the group. "You have all seen how clumsy they are. A webbed foot could not inflict that kind of damage."

The group of crows all sat back on their branches in silence, considering the truth to that statement.

Lustre tightened in his place, his innards curdling as he cursed in his mind that useless hunk of muscle Boughbend.

Cracks scooped up a circular piece of birch bark on to his head and let it fall over his eyes. He pawed blindly at the air, moving straight towards Lustre.

"My crown! My crown! Someone has toppled my crown! Help! I can't see. Where is the queen?" Cracks pawed around foolishly in a circle.

Lustre gritted his beak. With an uncustomary loss of composure, he batted the birch-bark crown off of Cracks's head with an angry swat.

"Yes, where is the queen?" "We want the queen!" 'Where is she?" "We need our queen!" erupted in a burst from all the crows in the trees.

I will kill that jester as he sleeps, seethed Lustre, his claws squeezing deep into the earth where he stood.

He had completely lost control. Lustre could do nothing but wait for several minutes for the din to subside.

"Our queen!" "Bring us the queen!" "She must be found!" "Summon the queen!!!"

Careen watched anxiously as she saw Lustre trembling, ever so slightly, with frustration. She knew it was not her place to say anything on the court floor, but she couldn't stand idly by and watch her love be humiliated like this.

When she felt like she could be heard, she shouted out in a strong, clear voice, "Has she gone to the Hollowing Tree?"

You stupid girl.

Lustre's eyes shot daggers towards Careen. She crumpled with hurt, thinking he would have been appreciative of her bravely crossing the line for him.

"The Hollowing Tree!" "The Hollowing Tree!" "She must be there!" shouted the masses.

"Ahem!" shrieked the princess, flapping her wings to get everyone's attention.

The crows settled.

"It has been three days, Lustre. Don't you think we should go check just to find out?" asked the princess in a nasally voice.

Lustre straightened his feathers. "It is *very* uncustomary, m'lady, to disturb the monarch on their sojourn. Plus, a king or queen always announces their plan to visit the Hollowing Tree to the group. But if that is what you think is best—" He gave a deep bow and extended his wing in a slow, grand wave to the ground. "—then by all means."

"Good. Do it, then," she snipped.

Lustre sat up with a jolt. Despite Lustre hinting several times at how it would be prudent for him to know it, the queen had never yet told him her name.

He certainly did not want the rest of the group to know this.

"Perhaps Boughbend, as her trusted protector, is a more appropriate choice?" he asked as sweetly as he could.

"I have never been made privy to the queen's name, sire," Boughbend responded.

Good. Lustre's competitive nature flickered with a surge of joy. He was never quite sure if the queen considered Boughbend to be Higher Crow than him or not. She seemed to enjoy his company so much more.

But in truth, this was bad. Now he had no one to foist the mission off on.

"Naturally," Lustre said condescendingly. "How silly of me."

Boughbend burned with rage. *You haughty crow, do as your princess commands. Now!* He would have said it out loud and given Lustre a swift peck to the forehead, but he knew it would not please the queen. All he could do was lock eyes with him and puff up his chest.

Lustre stiffened. If Boughbend ever turned on him, he knew he was no match for his strength. Lustre's only defence would be to fly as high as he could, and that might be seen as a sign of weakness and cowardice to the other crows. Plus, he would have to come down at some point.

Lustre smiled his most charming smile and turned back to the princess.

"My lady, I am all too happy to oblige your every wish. But since the Hollowing Tree is a sacred space reserved for royalty, don't you think it best that you, the princess, be the one to disturb the queen's peace?"

"But I don't know her name either," she whined.

"Huh?" A collective hushed inhalation of surprise spread across the tree line.

Lustre's heart dropped. *Even the princess doesn't know it.* All eyes turned to him.

"Only the Highest Crows can know!" cackled Cracks, hopping up and down, waving his head side to side, flapping his untidy wings. He did a backwards somersault, cackling with glee. "Only the Highest Crows!"

"Only the Highest Crows can know!" chanted the crows in the trees, escalating in volume. "Only the Highest Crow!" they screamed in a frenzied rallying chorus to Lustre to go get their queen.

"WAIT!" bellowed Lustre, pointing his powerful wingtip straight up to the sky.

The agitated mass hushed, waiting on his word.

He lowered his wing slowly to point directly at Cracks. Lustre's eyes narrowed into slits. "Not until this lowest of the Low, no-good gull of a crow has been sufficiently punished for insulting our princess! How dare he belittle Her Highness?!"

With all the talk of gulls, war, and hierarchy, the chanting had worked the crows up into a fever pitch. They quickly forgot they had been shouting the same insult and looked angrily down at Cracks.

"Yeah!"

"HE EVEN SAID HE WANTED TO BE KING! He has sullied the throne with his dirty claws. GET HIM!!!" yelled Lustre in his fiercest, most commanding voice.

Hundreds of crows soared out of the trees immediately, swooping down in a blind rage, beaks and claws eagerly extended for war.

"Oh dear!" said Cracks as he took lift and flapped as fast his straggly wings could carry him through the trees towards the Hollowing Tree.

Cracks!

Elsa covered her eyes as several strong young crows veered by, pecking at him viciously.

But Cracks was surprisingly acrobatic. He turned and dodged erratically, evading them, flying low into a grove thick with branches and brush.

When Elsa opened her eyes to see, he was ahead of them, darting and weaving randomly at high speed through the many thin trees. His attackers bonked clumsily into the obstacles and got their wings caught up in the brush.

"GET HIM!" boomed Lustre, in swift pursuit.

More crows swooped in to add to the charge. They awkwardly made their way through the thick wood as Cracks zipped and flitted unpredictably. More yet flew up and over the wood to cut him off when he came out into the clearing.

"Get him!" "Get him!" shouted crows hungrily from all directions. "Get that nasty Low Crow!"

Boughbend urged the princess to follow him. As much as he disdained the jester's shenanigans, he knew the queen was very fond of Cracks. She would be heartbroken if he were to be hurt seriously. It was Lustre that Boughbend wanted to keep an eye on. How far was this going to go?

Elsa turned and raced down the path for the Hollowing Tree. When she burst out onto the crossroads of paths in the clearing, crows were flying everywhere in a wild mess. It was difficult to see which one was Cracks.

Lustre saw the red-headed girl right away and broke from the group to scare her off. He swooped close and fast and from above, hoping if he kept her disoriented, she wouldn't be able to identify him later, if she was indeed the queen's spy.

Or perhaps she's Cracks's spy?

By now the whole group had gathered around the clearing. Many hovered and shouted support from the sidelines. Others sat on high tree branches in silence, disgusted at the sight of crows turning on another crow. Some even shouted desperately for it all to stop. But hundreds of crows now surrounded Cracks, each fighting to try to get a scratch or peck in for themselves.

Elsa batted away the attack from above. Lustre's claw cut her hand. She didn't seem to flinch. She moved closer to the horde around Cracks.

"Stop! Don't hurt him! He's just looking out for you," she shouted at the writhing mass in the air. It buckled and twisted around Cracks like a shoal of fish.

Lustre turned wing to fly upwards. That was when he saw it. He shuddered all through his body when he saw the emblem of the shiny around Elsa's neck.

What could this mean? How could our queen entrust such a treasure to a lowly, lowly human?

Cracks dipped and evaded as he was pecked at voraciously by the other crows. He quickly realized that only so many could get to him at one time and he started using them to block each other. He twisted and dropped, flying so unpredictably that it lessened the damage.

"*Yooo-hoooo!*" He flew by Elsa and gave a mischievous little wink as he passed. "Don't worry, Elsa!"

Elsa had to duck quickly to avoid the pelting of crows that followed. He swooped up, doing a loop-de-loop to get them away from her and to add insult to injury.

Who knew he could fly like this? wondered Boughbend. *We've all judged him by his shabby wings.*

Boughbend, the princess, and her ladies took a perch with a good view, in the highest elm.

"Get him! Get that miserable Low Crow mess!" screeched the princess at the top of her lungs, swept up in the fervour.

This rallied the combative energy of the group. With permission to cheer, Breezy and Careen added their shrill voices to the cacophony of taunts.

Lustre flew deep into the cluster of attacking crows. "NOW!" he boomed. "GET OVER HIM AND AIM DOWN."

Suddenly the angry horde thought to work as a group. Elsa watched with dread as they pecked and clawed at Cracks, forming a thick mass above him.

Boughbend tensed, readying himself to fly straight into the frenzy to prevent them from pecking Cracks to death once he was pinned.

Cracks bore his beak down straight at the ground and dropped out of the sky.

No. Don't go down. You'll be trapped! thought Elsa.

At the last second, Cracks swooped parallel with the ground. He turned with a grin at Elsa and shouted, "I like your necklace!" as he soared straight into the Hollowing Tree and disappeared.

Hundreds of crows crashed into the tree with a flurry of bonks. Three flapped in a panic in the hollow itself.

Lustre reared up and lifted up over the clearing. A hush fell over the whole group.

How did the lowest of Low Crows know the queen's name?

The weight of realization that things are not always as they seem sank in.

"But only the Highest Crows can know!" exclaimed the princess, whining her and everyone else's thought aloud.

Lustre almost screeched with frustration.

I'm losing them. Something must be done.

Elsa fell over laughing. "Ha ha! Don't you see? High Crow isn't about who sleeps in the highest tree. You are all being Low Crow right now. High Crow is about seeing things with a broader vision and taking everyone into account."

The crows pondered her words. Most had never thought in this way.

She's right, thought Boughbend.

Lustre's blood boiled. "Look at her shiny!" he bellowed. "She is a spy for the KING OF THE GULLS!"

Elsa looked down at the crowned, winged heart on her

chest. So did the rest of the group.

Lustre tilted his beak and pulled his wings back for attack. "GET HER!!"

He swooped down for her, followed by hundreds of crows still hungry for war. The rest of the group followed to see what would happen. Mass attack on a human had never occurred in their collective group memory.

Elsa followed Cracks's lead and ran into the thickest area of wood to deflect them. She ducked and weaved as they tried to get close enough to peck and scratch at her.

In the chaos of the chase, Lustre veered up and over the wood and looked around. The group was caught up entirely in the spectacle of the hunt.

Now is my chance, he thought. *If I disappear now, they will all think I followed Cracks into the Hollowing Tree. That is my only recourse.*

As fast and silently as he could, Lustre flew across the river for the countryside.

Elsa broke out of the woods and onto the main path leading out of the park. Several dogs barked at the mass of crows pursuing her. She ran panting into the washroom by the ball field and slammed the door.

The group hovered over, cawing wildly. Some even pecked at the window. But without Lustre to egg them on, they eventually lost their thirst for blood and circled back to court to regroup.

"Where is Lustre?" asked the princess, sinking down onto the throne.

The crows all looked around the branches, panting amongst themselves, hearts pounding.

"He must have followed Cracks into the Hollowing Tree," announced Careen in a confident voice.

She is becoming bold, thought Boughbend.

"Ah, yes," said the princess. "That makes sense."

"Hear, hear!" agreed the group, settling their ruffled feathers.

Boughbend lifted up out of the clearing to scan the horizon in all directions. He couldn't be sure, but he thought he saw a black bird flying low, far on the country side of the river. It seemed too small to be a raven.

Elsa rinsed the cuts and scratches on her arms in the sink. They were mostly from the trees, but there was a deep one on her hand from a crow. She washed it with soap.

She tucked her necklace under her shirt and timidly peeked out from under the roof of the building. The coast was clear. She could hear caws from the court.

Elsa made a break for it and ran all the way home.

CHAPTER 7

When Elsa burst through the door, Claire jolted up on the couch.

"Oh, sorry," said Elsa, feeling bad to have woken her.

"It's okay," said Claire. "I've got lots to do today." She yawned.

"But it's your day off," protested Elsa. "You should have some fun."

"Day off?" asked Claire sarcastically. "What's that?"

"*Fuh-un?*" taunted Elsa in a deep, silly voice. "What's that?"

Claire gave a begrudging little grin, rubbing her eyes. Her brow furrowed when she sat up.

"What happened to your arms?"

"Oh," said Elsa, looking down at the cuts and scratches, "I was just running in the woods."

Distract.

"Seriously, though, don't you think you should take some time for yourself today? Let loose a little," suggested Elsa.

In truth, Elsa was a bit worried about Claire. She was looking paler, thinner, and more haggard every day. Her tight little shoulders were almost up to her ears.

Claire looked at the pile of unfinished work on the table.

"Don't you have a friend you could call? Go for a coffee or something?" Elsa stared at her with that blank look she used on Ms. Witherspoon when in a standoff.

Claire bristled a bit. It was true that she had drifted from friends and fun of late.

"You're right," she sighed. "It's been a while since I went for a run."

While Claire got changed, Elsa put a bandage over the deep cut and ate a bowl of cereal. She contemplated her next move. She wanted to go back to the Hollowing Tree to look for Cracks, but now she needed a disguise.

Claire returned in running clothes and joined her for a bowl of cereal. They both ate in a brooding silence. Claire's heart seemed heavy. Elsa's was, too.

What if I never see Cracks again? It's been three days since Mom went into the hospital. When is Claire going to say something? Why doesn't anybody ever tell me anything?

Elsa was feeling angry now. Claire seemed to sense it.

"After my run, do you want to come with me to see Gran?"

"Really?" groaned Elsa. Those visits were always awful.

A few years back, Gran had assaulted someone while in the throes of one of her "episodes." The courts had dealt with it by placing her in a constant care home with other mentally ill seniors. Elsa couldn't stand the vibe of the place and Gran often said something harsh that made everyone feel uncomfortable.

"We'll be quick, I promise. I hate it there, too, but she's my mom. I feel guilty if I don't drop in once and a while."

"But you were just there yesterday."

"That was to speak with the administrator, about..." Claire drifted off, with a tense look on her face. "Well, Gran was stirring up trouble again. Anyway, they've got her fully medicated now." There was a hint of resentment in her voice. "She'll be easy to deal with today, I'm sure of it."

Elsa sat back in her chair and pouted. She stared blankly at Claire.

Why aren't we talking about my mother?

"And then after that you can come to the hospital with me," sighed Claire. "We should be able to talk to a doctor today."

"Okay," said Elsa, staring down at her empty bowl.

After Claire left for her run, Elsa went upstairs to change all her clothes. She pulled her hair into a ponytail and tucked it up into a hoodie. She even grabbed a pair of sunglasses. She opted to leave her blue fall coat at home.

Entering the park, Elsa could see the crows had dispersed to seek their food for the day. She passed one perched on a garbage can close by and felt her heart begin to race. The crow was so caught up in picking through the garbage it hardly noticed her.

Her heart jumped into her mouth when another crow landed just a few paces in front of her. It tilted its head and stared at her with empty reptilian eyes, then started pecking at the ground.

They don't recognize me.

Elsa breathed a sigh of relief and quickened her pace towards the Hollowing Tree.

She waited self-consciously while a family strolled by with their dogs. After they passed, she removed her sunglasses and stuck her head in the hollow.

"Cracks!" she whispered. "Can you hear me?"

The wind blew through the holes in the tree. She thought she heard the faintest "*Yooooo-hoooo!*" but discounted it as the wind.

Elsa leaned on the edge of the hollow and pondered. A queen would have a High Crow name. "Seer," she whispered. "Vantage. Knower. Big Picture."

No. It would be something beautiful, too. "Skyview. Wind-follow. Allsight. Visionary," she tried again. It was no use.

She looked out to check for crows. A sweaty, winded Claire jogged up the path.

"Oh, hey!" she breathed.

"Hi."

"I was just about to head back," smiled Claire, looking more rosy, luminous, and relaxed than she had all week.

Elsa was glad. She smiled an impish grin. "Race ya!"

Claire smiled back and lurched ahead dramatically. The race was on! Elsa darted to catch her. As she left the tree, the lip of the hollow grabbed a lone red hair that had been stuck to the hoodie.

Lustre squeezed the life out of the field mouse and ate joylessly. He noticed Elsa's dried blood on his claw. He scraped some flakes off with his beak and breathed them up into his mouth. It was delicious.

I'd like to taste her eyes.

A hint of the smell of country fox wafted over the wind. Lustre stiffened. He was vulnerable here on the ground.

Lustre lifted up into the air.

"*Krrrkkkkkll, Krrrlllllkkkkk*," hissed a raven, coming out of nowhere.

Two more teamed up with him and they darted and tossed, pecking at Lustre in the air.

"Get out of here, City Crow!" one shouted.

"Begone, garbage eater!" threatened another.

Lustre tried to get up above them, but they were too big and powerful. The largest of the three ravens came swooping in and gave him a hard slash to his wing.

"*Carrawwwk!*" screamed Lustre in pain. He watched as a clump of wing-feather fell from his beautiful shiny wing. His wing bone seared with hot agony. He felt blood falling. He couldn't fly with as much control.

The ravens continued their attack. "You are not welcome here, garbage eater!" He flinched away as they pecked within a feather's width of his neck.

Lustre dropped the mouse as an offering and swooped away. The ravens gave up the chase.

Lustre landed, heart pounding, to get a closer look at his wing. The missing feathers would leave a permanent gap.

I'll look like Cracks! he lamented woefully.

Suddenly a fox pounced. Lustre barely escaped with his life. Despite the sting, he flapped as hard as he could to take refuge in a nearby old barn.

I hate the country, he seethed.

"Did ya get my smokes?" demanded Gran.

Claire shook her head quietly.

"Well, what good are ya, then?" Gran shouted angrily with wild eyes.

Elsa sank into the chair, trying to melt into the wall.

Gran waved an arm in her direction. "Who's this ugly critter?" she yelled.

Claire closed her eyes with frustration. "Mom, this is Elsa. She's grown quite a bit since last time, hasn't she?" Claire tried to smile.

"Ugly as her mother," Gran grunted under her breath, fidgeting in her bed. She turned back to Claire. "I told you, I NEED cigarettes. What kinda daughter ya call yerself, anyway?" she uttered gruffly.

"One who's got to get going," said Claire through tight lips. "C'mon." She motioned to Elsa. "Bye, Mom. Enjoy yourself."

"I'll be glad once you folks are gone!" shouted Gran harshly from the room as they walked down the hall.

Claire marched faster, grabbing Elsa to follow pace. The fresh air felt good as they burst through the doors.

"That's the medicated version?" asked Elsa as they walked to the car.

"I'm sorry to have put you through that," said Claire, fishing through her messy purse for her keys. "Are you sure you want to come to the hospital? It might be more of the same."

Elsa just nodded stoically.

"All right," sighed Claire.

They drove in silence for a long time. Elsa was brooding

about what might happen. More and more knots formed in her stomach. She needed to think of something else.

"It must have been hard for you growing up."

Claire raised her eyebrows to herself and kept driving.

"She wasn't always like that. She could be really fun when she was up," she said after a while. "Creative. Funny. She'd let us do silly things like eat spaghetti in the bathtub and stuff. But the depression hollowed her out, the addictions, the bad choices…the meds…She's stable now, but she's a shell of the woman she used to be." Claire paused carefully and then said, "And she could be very harsh with us."

Claire cast a glance at Elsa as they turned in to the hospital. Elsa kept staring straight ahead.

"You know you can tell me anything, right, Elsa?"

Elsa looked down in her lap with a little nod.

She's wondering if Mom has been violent.

Claire wasn't the only one. There had been talk at school in the past as well. Psychologists. A social worker dropped by once. They all spoke to Elsa in high-pitched baby talk that made her want to throw something at the wall. She had duped them all. Claire wouldn't be so easy. Elsa knew she wouldn't be able to lie to her.

"It isn't a betrayal," assured Claire.

Distract.

"Do you think you'll ever have kids?"

"God, no!" Claire responded immediately. "Who would want to join this crazy family?" she said with a laugh.

Elsa gave an awkward smile, but inside her heart sank.

Claire doesn't want a child.

"Okay," said Claire, taking a big breath as they pulled up into the parking lot. "Let's go get your mum."

They waited for a long time. Nurses ambled past. Orderlies pushed people in wheelchairs. Fluorescent light bulbs hummed. At last the doctor approached Claire and asked her to join him over at the main desk.

Elsa wanted to come, too, but Claire's body language said stay put.

Nobody tells me anything!

She watched them converse in hushed voices down the hall. Elsa couldn't make out what was being said, but Claire seemed to become tenser and more upset. The doctor maintained his air of firm professionalism as she grilled him with questions. At last she threw up her hands. She stormed down the hall briskly.

"Let's go. They are keeping her."

"What?!" exclaimed Elsa, jumping up to keep pace. "But I want to see her!"

"I know. But they say it's a 'bad time.'" Claire was angry, but she kept it very contained.

"But they can't just keep her!" shrieked Elsa.

"Actually, they can. It's called a Form 1B. They can hold her for thirty days, whether she likes it or not."

"But why?"

"Because freedom becomes a slippery deal once mental

health is involved," said Claire in a monotone. "They have the right to keep her against her will because she threatened to jump."

"But when can I see her?" pleaded Elsa, double-timing her steps to keep up with Claire's brisk march.

Claire stopped and turned to her. "Soon," she said, softening. "We can visit her soon."

"But doesn't she want out?" asked Elsa quietly.

"They say she wants to stay for a while."

Elsa fought back tears.

"She just needs time, Elsa," soothed Claire.

Elsa bolted ahead of her in the parking lot. She ran towards a group of gulls.

"*Caw!*" she shrieked, spreading her arms wide, releasing a burst of rage at the birds.

The gulls picked up and flew away in fear.

The princess sobbed in little sniffs on the branch where she perched.

"What's wrong, m'lady?" asked Breezy tenderly.

"What if Lustre doesn't come back?" whimpered the princess.

"He will," assured Careen.

"But what if he doesn't come back tonight?" she whined.

Breezy and Careen exchanged a knowing look.

"I'm sure you'll do a fine job choosing the roost," ventured Breezy.

"But I don't know what to do!" protested the princess.

"Don't worry," said Careen. "If you can't decide, fly over to my right and I'll choose for you and you can follow me. No one will know."

Breezy's eyes almost popped out of her head. Careen glared at her.

"Are you sure?" sniffed the princess.

"Of course I'm sure," said Careen, wrapping her wing around the princess to comfort her. She motioned firmly to Breezy with her head.

Breezy quickly joined them, stroking the Princess's head with her wing.

"Everything will be fine," said Careen, soothing the princess, but staring straight at Breezy.

It was a sullen, silent ride home. When they pulled up to the house, Claire turned to Elsa.

"How about pad thai tonight?" She knew it was Elsa's favourite. Plus, Claire didn't have the gumption to cook anything right now.

"I just want to go for a walk by myself," Elsa said angrily.

"Okay," said Claire. "I'll go pick something up. Meet you back here."

Elsa slammed the car door and didn't look back.

Claire ran her hands through her hair and rested her forehead on the steering wheel for a moment. She felt helpless and unable to console Elsa. Watching her little body trudge down the street, Claire pulled away for the take-out.

Elsa pulled up her hoodie and walked to the park. The sunset blasted radiant gold, pink, and orange, but she was too angry to see it. She kicked a pop can.

"*Arrrrrr!*" she belted, running wildly down path to the Hollowing Tree.

Elsa found an old rotten log and smashed it against the tree. She bent down to overturn a big rock that was cradled in the earth. As she wrenched it from its place, her hood fell back.

Above, Careen was about to guide the group down into her favourite stand, the trees that faced the court on one side and the tennis court road on the other. She saw the red-haired girl and changed course.

"The girl!" she screeched. "The gull spy! Get her!"

The princess just naturally followed Careen without thinking, so relieved that someone else was taking the lead. The group followed the princess.

Many of the young crows, still hot with lust for war from earlier, keenly took up the chase.

"Take her out!" "Get her for the queen!" they shouted.

Elsa looked up from her madness to see the whole group barrelling down toward her.

Fear has a way of making anger disappear instantaneously. She bolted for the woods.

Hundreds of crows followed her, getting closer. She tripped on a log, but it helped her evade the first attacker and she went with it, turning it into a somersault and then continuing the run.

Cracks would have liked that.

She darted and weaved through the dark wood, but the crows had caught up. She covered her head as they scorched past with extended claws and fierce beaks.

Many others followed over top of the trees, shouting taunts from above and dropping feces.

Ruffle and Popcan hung back, looking at each other uncomfortably. This was someone's fledgling, too.

"The gulls can't have our park!" screeched Billow.

"Aim for her eyes!" howled Wrapper, in hot pursuit.

"Call them back!" Boughbend shouted to the princess. "They have no authority!"

But the princess found it all so exhilarating, "Get that lowly girl!" she shrieked.

"Get her for our queen!" added Careen with all her might.

Boughbend shuddered inside. This was the opposite of everything the queen stood for.

Elsa drew them towards the river, but then quickly reversed course back towards the Hollowing Tree. The crows lost ground on her, having difficulty slowing down and turning around in the dimming light, thwarted by trees. When Elsa burst back into the clearing, many of the hovering crows felt compelled to join in the attack.

"Now!" "She's getting away!" They pulled wings in and aimed beaks down at her.

She turned again but saw the mass of black advancing at her from the woods. She was trapped between the two forces!

All of a sudden, she seemed to leave her body. It was as if

her soul hovered high above her body over the clearing and time slowed down. She could see herself panicking as the two waves of black advanced in slow motion on either side, squeezing the space between her and the Hollowing Tree.

And then it popped into her head.

Instantaneously, she was back in her body and she knew exactly what to do. She ran at full speed at the Hollowing Tree and leaped. As her head entered the hollow, she whispered the name.

"Vista."

Her body continued to soar forward into space. Instead of smashing her head into the back of the hollow, she zoomed through a rose-purple sky with a silver-blue ocean lapping below her. The breeze was gentle and warm.

She was flying!

She stretched out her arms and laughed. It felt amazing. All the tension began to melt out of her body as she soared, chest open, parallel to the water.

"*Yooooo-hoooo!*" she heard to the side of her. She turned to look.

"Cracks!" she beamed. "What's happening?"

"We're hollowing!" he said with a broad smile.

The wind lifted them. They flew side by side at high speed.

Cracks swooped up, doing a loop-de-loop. "C'mon!" he urged her.

Elsa willed herself to follow him. She did a perfect loop-de-loop, too.

"This is incredible!" she glowed, doing somersaults, flips,

and twists through the air, continuing along the ocean surface.

The water and sky shimmered with an electric sparkle expanding as far as the eye could see.

"We all come from an egg and need the wind to fly," grinned Cracks, flying by playfully.

Elsa giggled, realizing it was true for humans, too.

"Become one with it," he said.

She closed her eyes and drew her palms to her sides. She felt herself zoom along, completely supported by the wind. She couldn't remember feeling this relaxed and safe.

"Surrender yourself completely," she heard him say.

As she breathed she felt herself expand into the sky, the edges of her skin losing their border and joining into the electrified expanse of calm beauty.

Without opening her eyes, she saw Cracks dip his beak and he soared straight down into the water and disappeared.

Erased of doubt, anger, and all things "Elsa," she followed suit, with no fear of what might happen or how she would get back.

Her body tipped upside-down and her face breached the surface of the water. As it entered, she suddenly burst right-side up out of a small pool by a mossy glade surrounded by soft, leafy trees. Her body rose up gently into the air and then slowly settled on the ground.

Cracks stood beside Elsa, shaking off his feathers. "Welcome. Welcome, dearie."

Just beyond him sat the queen.

"I guess you need no introduction, since you already know

her name," Cracks giggled happily.

"Hello, Elsa," she said with a warm smile. Her luminous black eyes sparkled and her soft matte black feathers reflected the warm golden light all around them.

Elsa found herself falling to her knees in the moss. "It's a great honour, Your Majesty," she managed to stammer, with her head bowed low.

The queen laughed. "No need for formalities here. Come sit next to me, girl. I am so glad you've made it.

Elsa scrambled up the mossy mound and sat comfortably at the queen's feet.

"I have something to show you, my dear," whispered Vista joyfully.

The queen lifted her soft wing to reveal a pure white baby crow.

"Ah, so cute! I guess this is why you needed to leave?"

"Aye," the queen nodded.

Elsa looked down at the tiny fledgling. His eyes were black, but all of his feathers, beak, and feet were completely white.

"Crows don't normally give birth at this point in the season, so I knew he would be special."

His full eyes seemed bright and aware. He held his body with great strength, despite his young age. He looked deep into Elsa's eyes and seemed to smile as if he had known her forever.

"Now, if we can just get past all this hating someone because they are different business, I know in my heart of hearts he will be our next king."

This is going to be a problem with the pale-feather-hating crows.

"Aye," said the queen, a twitch of sadness in her tone, as if she had heard Elsa's thought. She smiled again as she stroked her son's back tenderly with her wing.

"So," said the queen, looking at him with great love, "we have decided to name him Cirrus."

"We?" said Elsa with great surprise, turning to Cracks.

Cracks puffed up his chest with a proud smile and a mischievous little wink.

"Congratulations to you both!" said Elsa with a great big smile. "But if he will be king, how come you are telling me his name?"

"Only the Highest Crows can know, my dear," said Cracks, looking proudly at her.

Elsa was at a loss for words.

"We loved what you said by the Hollowing Tree," said the queen.

"You can hear through it?" Elsa wondered.

"When you are one with the wind, you know all it knows." Vista waved her wing towards the pool of water.

A breeze rippled over the surface. As the water stilled, it showed Lustre huddled on a barn beam, looking miserable.

The queen waved her wing again. The pool rippled and changed to reveal the group of crows, panting and stunned, gathered by the Hollowing Tree. Boughbend stood in the middle and addressed the group.

"It seems we have been looking at this all wrong. Darkness

is upon us now. Let us take our roost," he said humbly.

The group picked up and followed Boughbend in a daze of shock.

The queen looked back at Elsa. "Cirrus still needs some time to strengthen." Then she looked at Cracks with a smile. "And my lovely mate's wounds will heal more quickly here."

Cracks beamed rays of adoration towards Vista and the boy.

"The dawn after tomorrow, I want you to return to the court and sit on the throne."

"Me?" asked Elsa, confused.

"Be my interim queen and try to influence their hearts to a Higher level. We are all in great danger now."

Elsa breathed in the weight of the assignment.

"Boughbend is almost there. He will listen and help support your efforts. The others will want to have the Hollowing described to them, but, of course, what happens here can't be described in words, it can only be experienced. You must lead by example and they must figure it out for themselves."

Elsa swallowed. She wasn't sure she was up for such a challenge.

"Just keep your head, Red," tutted Cracks in his usual scratchy tone.

"It's soon time for you to return, Elsa," said Vista softly.

Elsa grasped the necklace around her neck. She knew crows liked shiny things.

"Please accept this gift from me," she said, taking it off and placing it humbly in the moss at the queen's feet.

"Keep it, my darling. You have given me true shine and that

is all I need. Cracks and I have worked for seasons to teach our crows the real meaning of High Crow and Low Crow. You are the first to see past the small way of looking at things and learn to perceive in this other way. It gives us strength to continue in this difficult time."

The queen bent down and picked up the necklace with her beak. She lifted it up into the air and inserted her wing tip to open the circle of chain. She placed the necklace gently over Elsa's head and settled back down on the moss by her son.

"Keep it to remember what kind of shine has the most value. Even though you know my name, the Hollowing Tree won't let you pass if you slip back into Low Crow thinking."

CHAPTER 8

Elsa awoke in darkness, curled on the couch. She had no memory of how she got there.

A plate of pad thai sat cold on the coffee table. She realized she was hungry and ate in the dim stillness.

She climbed the stairs and saw Claire lying stiffly in her mother's bed. Elsa slipped into her own and drifted back into a dreamless sleep.

Elsa was sullen and withdrawn the next day at school. She doodled a sketch of Cracks with his wings spread wide, two feathers missing. Ms. Witherspoon picked on her with snippy questions all morning. Elsa could barely get her voice to work as she answered them, not looking up from her drawing.

At recess, she leaned against the wall. She continued to detail the picture of Cracks.

Breagh, Gabby, and Lenore passed by and gawked at the cuts and scratches on her arms.

"Do you think she's a cutter?" Breagh said, purposely loud enough for Elsa to hear. "I hear some crazy girls cut themselves just so they can feel something."

The mean girls turned back to see if she'd heard.

"I can think of something I'd like to cut," said Elsa in a cold, flat tone, not even looking up.

"Oh yeah?" taunted Breagh, "Like what? Your hair?"

Gabby snickered.

"You look as ragged as that crow of yours," sneered Lenore.

Elsa looked up with rage. She was sick to death of their bullying.

"Good. Because you know what a group of crows is called?" Elsa paused for added drama. She narrowed her eyes at them. "*A murder.*" She added a little crazy to her eyes for good measure. The girls scoffed, but she could tell that inside they were scared by the wildness she could conjure.

"Elsa! Look!" shouted Eh Ta Taw suddenly from the grass.

He pointed to a black fox with a white-tipped tail that scuttled down the street in broad daylight.

This broke the tension between the girls and they scuttled off as well. Elsa rose to join him.

In the past two years, the coyote population had risen in the countryside. This had pushed the foxes into the green spaces around the city, but they had soon figured out it was easier to find food amongst the human waste and they had moved right into town.

People had worried for their cats and small dogs when the foxes had first arrived, but so far an uneasy peace remained between the factions. It was now common to see the reddish-orange foxes periodically in the core of the city, even during the day. But it was still quite rare to see this black-and-white type, ironically called a silver fox, a genetic remnant of the fox-fur trade.

They watched quietly as the beautiful fox slithered by, crouched low in trepidation.

"You and me," said Eh Ta Taw after it had passed, "we are like that fox."

The recess bell rang and everyone made their way back into the school.

"What do you make of it?" asked Popcan of Ruffle, who was staring off at the field by the river. In the distance gulls squawked, fighting over an old ice-cream cone.

"I don't know what to think," sighed Ruffle.

"Lustre will tell us, once he returns from the Tree," said Careen loudly from a branch above. She said it partially to calm the lower crows, but also for the princess to hear.

"I hope he returns with my mother," said the princess to herself.

"Nobody actually saw him enter the Hollow," said Bough-bend sternly, but nobody seemed to listen.

"We should just declare war on the gulls right here and now!" cawed Wrapper.

"Hear, hear!" agreed many others all around.

"We should take one of their own at least!" howled Billow.

"For Berry!" "Berry!" "Berry!" a crowd chanted wildly.

"Stop your screeching!" screamed Ruffle, fluttering up into the sky before the trees. "If we stoop to killing their children out of spite, we are no better than *whoever* took my girl."

"She's right!" shouted Boughbend in a deep voice. "Silence this ugly song. You sound like a bunch of gulls."

Boughbend regretted that last comment as soon as it came out of his mouth. But it had done the trick. The crows were silent.

"Disperse," said the princess in a firm voice.

Boughbend gave her an approving smile.

Each took flight.

For the rest of the morning, Elsa couldn't stop thinking about the Karen boy and what he had said.

At lunch, she approached him in the schoolyard.

"What did you mean when you said we are like that fox?"

Eh Ta Taw looked out at the children playing around the schoolyard.

"We are different from the others, so we have to be careful not to get too brave."

"But you were brave when they bothered you and it scared them," reminded Elsa.

"Brave, but not too brave. I scared them just enough."

Eh Ta Taw kicked a little stone with his foot.

"The fox knows if it doesn't bother too much, then the city doesn't bother. But if he gets too wild, the humans won't tolerate him sharing the space."

Elsa understood that he was trying to warn her to keep a low profile. The mean girls became syrupy sweet and innocent when it came to manipulating the grownups.

"But doesn't it bother you that those girls are awful to you when you've been through so much?" she asked at last.

"They are children. I am happy for them they still get to be children."

Elsa was quiet. So was Eh Ta Taw. The other children

laughed and ran around them.

"They can't even imagine what we have known," Eh Ta Taw said, kicking at another stone. After a long silence, he looked at her with his straight spine and stern brow. "I don't know what you have been through, but a fox can sniff another fox before the people do."

It felt good to be recognized. She admired how unabashed he was about himself, despite all the setbacks he had faced. He was a warrior.

"My mother is in the hospital," revealed Elsa. *After beating me, neglecting me, and stealing from me!* "She has a mental illness. I have been keeping it a secret, but I was living on my own for a while, without any money or food."

Elsa felt pressure release. It felt good to admit at least some of it to someone.

Eh Ta Taw nodded thoughtfully, without judgement. "My father was killed in the resistance when I was very young. Uncle was like a father to me until he died two years ago. I was born in a camp in Thailand. I have never seen my homeland."

Elsa nodded quietly, feeling honoured he would share this with her. "I hope we can be friends," she said at last.

Eh Ta Taw's serious eyes brightened a little bit. He gave her the tiniest nod.

The lunch bell rang.

Elsa was happy to have made a friend, but talking of her mother had brought the heaviness of the situation back to the forefront of her mind. She festered while she was supposed to be working on a quiet writing assignment.

What if she doesn't want to come out? What if she doesn't want me back? Claire said she doesn't want children. What is going to happen to me?

Tension coiled in her stomach, twisting ever tighter. She felt like a balloon about to pop.

Plop! A crumpled piece of paper landed in front of her on her desk.

The mean girls silently celebrated their good aim while Ms. Witherspoon had her back turned, writing a paragraph out on the board.

Elsa glared at them and quietly opened the paper.

Inside was a VERY rude drawing of her naked on her back. Underneath it said:

Elsa loves black birds and brown boys.

Her rage surged to the breaking point and she popped. She stood up and hurled the crumpled note back at them. "*Caw!*" she shouted out, spreading her arms like menacing wings at them.

Ms. Witherspoon whipped around. "Elsa! What's going on?" she questioned sternly.

Gabby quickly covered the note with her foot.

"*Caw!*" screeched Elsa fiercely at Ms. Witherspoon. "*Caw! Caw! Caw!*" She flapped her arms, jeering at the whole class, with her neck jutted out.

Breagh, Gabby, and Lenore and the rest of the class couldn't believe what they were seeing. Eh Ta Taw looked away.

"*KrrrawwwllK!*" shouted Elsa one more time and she soared

out the door.

"Keep to your desks," said Ms. Witherspoon firmly to the other students and she chased down the hall after Elsa.

Claire shuffled through some papers on her messy desk. She held her phone to her ear with her shoulder while she rifled through some old receipts.

"I shipped it out last week, I'm sure of it," she said to the woman on the line, not sounding very sure. She flipped through the book of stubs. "It should have arrived..." She stalled, flipping some more.

She raised a finger to another woman who was waiting impatiently at the counter, signalling she just needed another minute. The customer sighed.

Claire cringed, realizing she had forgotten to ship this order. She deflated. It was supposed to be there by now.

"You're right." She sighed and grabbed the piece and started wrapping it hurriedly in tissue. "I have it right here...I'll ship it out today, priority post, okay?"

The phone beeped, signalling another call coming through. Claire pulled the phone away from her ear to see who it was. It was Elsa's school.

"Listen, I'm sorry, I've got to go. My kid's school is on the other line." Claire hung up on the disgruntled caller and signalled for just one more moment to the customer at the counter. The woman shifted her weight with a hint of disdain.

"Hello?" Claire answered.

"Is this Elsa Doran's emergency contact?"

"Yes, it is," said Claire with concern.

"You will have to come pick her up from school immediately."

"Why? What's wrong?"

"She is behaving like a crow and she won't stop."

Claire and Elsa burst out of the doors of the school. Both their brows were furrowed, lips tight. Elsa threw down her backpack at the car door.

"*Caw!*" she shouted angrily at Claire.

Claire sighed, her chest tight, shoulders high. She opened the car door. She had no time for this. "Get in," she said with little patience.

"*Krrak!*" bleated Elsa, thrusting out her neck and spreading her arms with ferocity to protest.

Claire held her ground. She gave Elsa the same blank stare that Elsa usually doled out.

Elsa harrumphed into the seat and threw down her backpack. Claire crossed to the driver's seat, shaking her head with frustration. Elsa rolled down the window furiously with a pout.

Inside the car, Claire steadied herself, trying to regain her even keel. "Elsa," she appealed gently, "why are you doing this?"

Elsa turned to look at her, with a birdlike flit of her head. Then she turned away again with the same dramatic gesture.

Outside, some crows cawed in a distant tree. Elsa looked up at them imploringly and cawed twice with a pathetic tone, as if to say, *Help. Save me!*

Claire rolled her eyes and they drove away.

When they pulled up to the government building, Claire filled with agitation. She had been questioned and "assessed" in this very same place as a child.

Elsa stared at her angrily.

"You got us into this mess," Claire said through gritted teeth. "You had better play along, for your own sake."

Elsa begrudgingly got out of the car and they walked in to present the sheet of paper the school had given them to the front desk.

Dr. Whittle, the child psychiatrist, showed them into a small room. It was painted in pastel shades, with children's drawings of rainbows and sunshine and families pinned all over the wall.

Elsa scanned the room quietly. There was a low table with blank paper and markers. A creepy faceless doll sat on a comfy-looking chair.

Dr. Whittle cast Claire a knowing look.

"I'll just be outside," said Claire nervously to Elsa. Elsa nodded.

Dr. Whittle was a tense bird of a woman. Elsa could tell she took great pride in being good at what she did. As she closed the door, Elsa sank down into the chair.

She doesn't even have a child, I bet.

The doctor crouched down on the floor across the table from her with a forced smile.

"Elsa?" She handed her a black marker. "Can you draw a picture for me?"

There was that high-pitched baby voice again. Elsa sighed and took the marker, resigned to her fate. Having been handed a black marker, of course she began to draw a crow. As she added the crown, Dr. Whittle leaned in with great interest.

They ate supper in silence. Claire seemed tired, peeved, and distracted. Elsa left a lot on her plate.

Without taking it to the sink, or saying goodnight, Elsa went to her room to sulk.

Lustre flew over the river in the cloak of darkness. Crows have poor night vision, so they avoid flying in true darkness. But he knew the river would be clear and he fumbled along by trust, carried by the wind. He felt comforted as he approached the glow of the city and the scattered lights of the park.

He made his way to the lip of the Hollowing Tree while the rest of the group slept. He whispered every royal name he could remember from studying the ancient songs. Nothing worked.

As he was about to give up, he felt a tickle at his foot. He snatched it firmly with his sharp beak and pulled, extracting a long, thick hair from between the splinters of wood. He flew up into the pink city light that reflected off the clouds. The hair was that unmistakeable shade of red. His eyes narrowed as he soared silently over the woods to set down atop the playground slide.

If the girl and the queen and Cracks are all in there conspiring together, I must make my move now or all is lost.

But what is my move?

Lustre took shelter in the rocks by the shoreline. He squeezed himself between some big craggy boulders; he knew the crows would never think to find him there. A little bit scared he might be found by a gull, he stayed up late into the night, scheming his strategy.

Having gone to bed so early, Elsa awoke before dawn. She grabbed her coat and crept silently out of the house.

The stone was cold and damp as she sat down on the throne in the dark.

It will be dramatic when they wake to find me here.

She hoped they would not try to peck her to death. She had her sunglasses in her pocket just in case.

She breathed, remembering the calm purple sky of the Hollowing to calm her nerves. The wind tickled at her face, reminding her she had its support.

At first hint of light the crows began to stir in the roost. Careen had selected her favourite stand of trees by the court and had hardly slept at the excitement of having had the taste of power. The rest of the crows thought it had been the princess's choice, of course, but she knew.

The night before, Careen had been disappointed when

Boughbend had simply flown up into the trees by the Hollowing Tree and everyone had followed. She was glad when he had ceded power back to the princess last night and the princess had flown to her right to signal she wanted her to make the choice.

I hope the queen never comes back. Careen tingled to herself as sun peeked over the horizon.

"News! I have news of your queen!" called Elsa.

Careen sat up with a burst of shock. So did the rest of the group.

Claire had had a fitful sleep. She lay awake early, fretting about everything. She rose to check on Elsa. She wasn't on the couch or in her bed.

Claire panicked. The authorities would be scrutinizing this household carefully. She needed to prove she could keep Elsa close and safe. After searching the house and yard, Claire ran down empty the street.

"Elsa!" she called desperately.

At the end of the street, Claire could hear the crows waking up in the park. She ran across the park road and passed the ball field.

"Elsa!" she cried.

"What's this?" "The girl has returned!" "She sits on our throne?" "What news of the queen?" The crows flitted and shouted in a tizzy.

"Let's hear her out!" bellowed Boughbend.

The crows quieted down. They had to admit they were curious.

"Your queen loves you all very much," said Elsa as nobly as she could. "She just needs some time and soon she will return to you."

"But why?" "Why did she leave us?" "She left us in danger!" "She abandoned us to the gull menace!" shouted many crows angrily from the trees.

"She is looking out for everybody," said Elsa, spreading her arms wide, "but you must find the generosity in your hearts to also let her take care of herself."

"But Berry!" "The gulls!" "We didn't know what to do!" "We were forsaken!" erupted the chorus of crows.

The crow chatter burst louder as Claire ran down the path. She scanned frantically through the criss-cross of bare, black branches. A pine bough scratched near her eye as she barrelled towards the din of the crows.

Then she stopped.

There in the distance was Elsa sitting on the rock by Dead Man's Pond.

"Caw! Caw! Caw!" called Elsa up to the crows in a loving tone.

A flood of relief sank through Claire's body. Then a flicker of anger coursed through her bones. She snuck up on Elsa quietly, from behind.

"Caw! Caw! Caw!" cooed Elsa up to the trees. She rose from the rock with arms spread and danced for the crows graciously.

Claire snatched her arm firmly. "Elsa!" she uttered in a harsh whisper.

Elsa looked shocked and then cowered slightly as if preparing to be hit.

Claire's anger melted.

"Elsa," she pleaded, "why are you doing this?"

Elsa looked up at the thousands of crows that surrounded them.

"They need a queen," she said plainly.

Claire felt all her breath release with the weight of that statement. She looked at this incredible girl and thought of all she had been through. Claire felt tears well up in her eyes, which she fought back.

"Are you ready to go see your mum?" she asked, trying to sound as supportive as she could.

Elsa gave a quiet little nod.

"Okay," said Claire, tenderly hooking her arm into Elsa's. "Let's hope she's ready to see us."

They walked homewards together.

Lustre had slept late, but the din awoke him. He listened to the crows' chorus and smiled a cold smile.

Now is my time.

He snuck out from between the rocks and took lift. The wind supported him up as he soared powerfully high. He watched the red-haired girl, with a big human, walking away from the agitated group of crows.

"DON'T BELIEVE HER LIES!" he boomed as he spiralled down onto the throne.

"Huh?" breathed in the collective mass. They silenced, all eyes on him.

His talons relished the click of the hard stone under his feet.

I love the way this feels.

The ward was stuffy and warm.

"Hearts," said Elsa, laying down a card to change the suit.

Claire played a card from her hand. They both looked up at Dana, who slouched on the far side of the couch, lost in her thoughts.

"Mum," said Elsa softly, "it's your turn."

Dana looked at her hand with disinterest and tossed a card down. It was a diamond.

Elsa and Claire shared an uncomfortable look. Elsa played a diamond to keep the game going. Claire followed her lead. They looked at Dana, who was gnawing at her cuticles.

"Mum?" asked Elsa gently.

Dana sighed and chucked a card down without even looking at what it was. She let the rest of her hand fall face-side-up on the table. Claire smouldered at her. Elsa put her cards down sadly.

A nurse arrived with a small plastic cup full of pills and a bigger cup of water. She placed them in front of Dana.

With shaky hands, Dana quietly swallowed one pill at a time.

Claire sighed and grabbed her coat. "Who wants to go for a

walk?" She stood up, shot a pressing look at Dana, and began to head outside.

Elsa picked up her coat and lingered, hoping to catch her mom's eye. Dana looked at her quickly, but then looked away. Elsa followed Claire, hoping her mother would join them.

It felt good to get out of the dreary feeling of the ward. The hospital was well placed, with peaceful grass and trees by the river. Elsa ran ahead of them as Dana shuffled with hunched shoulders and crossed arms. Claire ambled slowly at her sister's side.

"How's she doing at school?" asked Dana at last, somewhat halfheartedly.

"She really needs you, Dana."

"Claire." Dana bristled as if she had been attacked. "I'm not...I just..." She shook and brooded, her face pinched with anguish. Finally, she turned Claire and trembled, almost with begging with fragile desperation, "*I can't.*"

"Mom, look!" called out Elsa from ahead on the grass. She had collected two branches and held them out like wings.

Claire smiled warmly as Elsa danced in a circle, wings outstretched. Elsa's face dropped a bit when she completed her turn and saw Dana was staring off in the distance instead.

Can't she even pull it together enough to give her a little something while we're here? Claire broiled with anger, but then compassion took over. *She feels too ashamed to look at her.*

"Can we go down by the water?" Elsa asked her mother, full of hope.

Claire and Elsa waited for Dana's reaction.

"Mummy's getting cold," she said flatly and turned back for the hospital.

Elsa and Claire followed, feeling disappointed.

"I have been to the Hollowing Tree myself, and the girl is lying!" shouted Lustre.

The group listened intently.

"You have all been betrayed. The queen went there to take a secret meeting with the KING OF THE GULLS!"

"Wuh?!" shrieked the group in shock.

"She will return, telling you we must make peace with the gulls. But she is making an alliance with them! She is jeopardizing all that we have because she wants to have more birds to bring her shiny!" He flapped up from the throne to add emphasis, then landed again.

"No!" "She wouldn't!" "It can't be!" they shouted.

"Your queen has TURNED HER BACK ON US!" Lustre said with great relish.

"What happened to your wing?" asked Boughbend flatly.

Lustre looked down sorrowfully at his damaged plumage. *Might as well make this horrible scar work for me.* "I fought the king and his guards for you!"

Many crows burst into cheers.

It's working, thought Lustre.

"Now we must all fight to keep what is ours!" he commanded.

The cheers grew louder.

"The gulls will wait until we are all lulled by peace, then they will attack our young while we sleep!" Lustre flapped his wings vigorously, proud of the gap in his feathers now.

"Never!" "We must get to them first!" "They hate us for what we have!" The shouts continued to escalate from the trees.

"We must rid this park of HER AND HER HORRID GULLS ONCE AND FOR ALL!"

Some cheered voraciously. Others fell quiet. It was hard for them to contemplate turning on their queen.

Elsa crashed out the front doors of the sad old building. She thumped quickly down the stairs and turned back to Claire with a smouldering look.

"She's not coming home soon, is she?" Elsa's eyes burrowed angrily into Claire for answers.

Claire didn't have any. "I don't know," she mumbled helplessly.

They drove in silence to the government building.

After the preliminary consultation, the child psychiatrist had asked that they return for a more detailed analysis. Claire didn't like the sound of that, but had complied begrudgingly.

She fretted as she waited in the office, staring at all the diplomas on the wall. Elsa was with Dr. Whittle in the other room. It seemed to be taking a long time.

At last the door opened.

"Elsa," said Dr. Whittle, "I'd like to speak to Claire for a bit."

Dr. Whittle stepped into the office, closing the door. Elsa moved quietly to the door and bent down to put her ear to the crack at the bottom to eavesdrop.

"Psychotic!" exclaimed Claire incredulously.

"In the schizophrenic spectrum," said Dr. Whittle matter-of-factly as she wrote down a list of medications.

"She's a little girl!" protested Claire.

The doctor looked up from her prescription paper. "She thinks she's the *queen of the crows*, Claire," she said in a condescending tone.

"She's just trying to cope!" pleaded Claire.

Dr. Whittle finished her list and sat up with an air of authority. "Given your family history, I think it's best to start medications immediately." She pushed the paper across the desk curtly.

Claire's blood boiled, but she took the paper quietly.

Elsa feigned ignorance on the drive back. Claire seemed very troubled. She said nothing.

I hope she's not taking me back to school.

Elsa did not look forward to facing the mean girls and everyone else with so much on her mind. She relaxed a bit when Claire turned towards the house.

As they pulled up, Claire paused in the driver's seat.

"You'll have to go to school tomorrow, but why don't you take the rest of today off?"

Elsa nodded gratefully.

"I've got so much work to do. And I've been keeping such erratic store hours lately. It's really not great for business. You can come to the shop, if you want."

Elsa didn't really want to, and Claire could sense it.

"Do you mind hanging out here by yourself?" asked Claire apologetically, looking so frail and tired.

"No. I'd like to, actually," said Elsa. "I promise to stay put," she added.

Claire gave a little appreciative smile. "Do you think you can make your dinner, too? I might be late."

"No problem," said Elsa cheerily, trying to lighten Claire's load.

"Call me immediately if any social worker shows up. Better yet, just don't answer the door for anyone."

"Okay," said Elsa with assurance as she got out of the car.

"Okay," said Claire, looking a bit relieved. She paused, sitting in the car, looking like she was going to say something. Elsa lingered, waiting for the bomb to drop. But Claire just looked uncomfortable for a moment, then gave an awkward little smile and wave and pulled away.

We are such a hassle for her. Claire probably wishes she could be rid of us all.

Claire drove down the road, kicking herself for not saying "I love you."

There was much discussion during the day's dispersion. Crows clustered together in groups whispering amongst themselves.

"We could easily take out the gulls if we work together," boasted Wrapper.

"But what if the gulls of the park teamed up with the gulls of other shorelines?" asked Popcan.

"They outnumber us by ten thousand easily, if we count all the gulls, not just the ones that roost in the park," stated Whirly sombrely.

"But gulls are stupid and poorly organized," said Billow. "They are no match for our wits."

"So we assume," added Whirly.

"I want to hear what the queen has to say from her own beak," said Ruffle.

Lustre circled high, trying to get a feel for the sway of the group. He saw a group of young males who had clearly enjoyed the attack on Cracks. He spiralled down to join them on a soccer field.

"You are all brave fighters," he said as he landed. "Our crows will need your strength when the time comes."

The young males puffed up at the compliment.

"What was it like fighting the gulls?" asked Span.

"They are big and strong, but they lack our wisdom," responded Lustre. "If we work together, they are no match for us," he continued haughtily.

"We are with you, sir," said Curbside.

He fought hungrily in the fight, noted Lustre.

"We will fight, too," said Twilight as she landed with a bunch of formidable females.

"Of course," said Lustre with all his charm. "We must fly united."

All the youth nodded in agreement and smiled at each other.

"Disperse and spread the word to the others," Lustre commanded.

Boughbend flew on high alert all day. He had given the princess space to process her thoughts, but had kept a close watch on her. He wanted no crow taking this out on her.

Careen whispered to her while she sobbed a little on a fence.

Breezy returned with half a hot dog bun.

"How is the princess?" he asked.

"Not good," she answered with a troubled look. "It's a bit much for her to handle."

Boughbend ventured closer to the princess. "Forgive me, my lady, but keep in mind that not one of us saw Lustre enter or come out of the Hollowing Tree. He could have hidden in the country and been attacked by ravens for all we know."

Careen stiffened. The princess sniffed, straightening up a bit.

"I know this is all very troubling for you, but try to take heart. We won't know the truth until the queen returns."

"Thank you, Boughbend," said the princess. She wiped her tears and accepted the bun from Breezy.

Careen sat back quietly.

Elsa decided to clean the entire house. There wasn't much

more she could do to be helpful to Claire. As she dusted and tidied, she tried not to relive the scene at the hospital. It was difficult.

She scrubbed the nooks and crannies behind the toilet. It was disgusting. She relived the moments at school in her mind.

Am I psychotic?

She wished they had the Internet at the house so she could figure out what that meant exactly.

She obsessed around the knob at the base of the toilet, trying to get all the bits of grime and hair. Each wipe removed some, but returned some others. It was difficult to get it perfect. She had seen her mother do this when she was on an upswing.

Elsa sat back, letting the few tiny flecks remain.

"Our queen would never betray us," said Sparkle.

"Things have changed on her watch," muttered Old Crow Beetle.

"She's lost sense of our High Crow ways, always preaching peace with those pathetic birds," agreed Bigworm, another elder.

Bigworm had felt slighted when she brought the queen a bottle cap, just before the big storm came last summer. The queen had hardly seemed to notice.

"We must wait and hear what she says before we form any opinions," piped up Gust, the oldest of them all.

That night's roost was a disjointed affair. The crows hovered awkwardly, not knowing if they were supposed to follow Lustre or the princess. The princess wasn't sure either. She flew to the right of Careen, unsure of what to do next. Careen looked to Lustre. He hesitated as well.

Oh, for soaring's sake, thought Careen, exasperated by their moment of weakness. She dove down, choosing the stand by the skate park.

Everybody followed.

There was much tuttering in the trees and it took a long time before the group went to sleep.

Elsa listened to the last of the caws settle as she put sweet potatoes on to boil. She checked on the tofu in the oven. It still needed a bit more time.

She had appreciated getting to know Claire's new weird food. Elsa had enjoyed the time they had spent in the kitchen together and she enjoyed the challenge of figuring out how to work with new ingredients.

While she waited, she decided she would vacuum the living room. As she pulled out the vacuum she knocked a pile of bills off a side table. A small thin envelope slipped out from between them.

Elsa saw it was addressed to her. It was her mother's handwriting, though it looked a bit shakier and more childish than usual. The postmark indicated she had sent it two days ago. Elsa went to open it, but then stopped. Why hadn't Claire given her this? Did Claire know what it said inside? Had her mother written to say she didn't want to take care of her anymore?

Had Claire just not seen it hidden between the bills?

The timer beeped on the stove.

Elsa stared at the unopened letter while she ate by herself.

Careen was awakened by the sound of the keychain hitting the branch beside her. She watched as it fell down and disappeared into the leaf litter below. She looked up and narrowed her eyes at Lustre's silhouette hovering high above her in the darkness. She took lift to follow him, high out over the river.

"You raided my stash," she whispered, a bit annoyed.

"You said the chain was mine," said Lustre snidely.

Careen couldn't argue with that. "Still, what a waste of good shiny."

"Oh, there will be plenty of shiny when you and I rule the park," Lustre cooed.

Careen tingled at the thought.

"How is the princess?" Lustre barked her out of her reverie.

"Well, I was doing great with her until Boughbend started filling her with thoughts that no one ever really saw you come or go from the Tree."

Lustre hoped she couldn't see his wince in the darkness.

"You did go, didn't you?" she asked, seeking reassurance.

Lustre just shrugged out his wings to emphasize the gap in the feathers.

"Boughbend said you could have just gone to hide in the country and been attacked by ravens."

That cursed oaf, he thought. "Careen, my darling, if you

want to be queenmate you must help me, not doubt me," he said as sweetly as he could.

That shut her up, thought Lustre with a flash of self-satisfaction.

"Now," he added coolly, "it is crucial that we have the princess onside when the time comes."

"And when is that?" she asked dutifully.

"Just follow my lead," he said with a deep chill in his tone.

"I'll do my best," gulped Careen. *It is her mother.*

They silently returned to where the others slept.

Elsa took the envelope with her to bed. She turned on her lamp and opened it.

Dear Elsa,

I've had a lot of time to think in here.
I have good days and bad days.
At first I was mad they were keeping me, but now I'm glad. I need a rest. I want to get better.
Going for days without sleep would make anyone go out of their right mind, but still, it's no excuse for what I have done to you.
I am ashamed of what I have put you through.
I am proud of you and your strength.
I hope you can find it in your heart to forgive me.
I know I have a lot to live for, the most important thing being winning back your trust.
I'll be home for Christmas...

Love,
Your Mum.

All the tears that Elsa had been holding onto for all this time flowed steadily down her cheeks.

She cried herself to sleep, but they were not tears of sadness. They were tears of joy.

Claire rubbed her eyes in the dark store. She set aside what she was working on. She wasn't making good progress anyway, with everything on her mind.

She pulled out the prescription paper, clicked on her computer, and searched the side effects of the first medication on the list.

Claire's chin began to quiver as she read. The side effects were serious. Some of them she recognized in her own mother, whom she knew took this pill as well.

She didn't know what to do.

Claire buried her head in her hands, feeling all the weight she had carried over all these years, trying to be the rock. At last, alone in her store, Claire allowed herself to crumble into sand.

"*Arrrrgrgghh!*" she screamed as she lurched out of the chair. She reached under the worktable and ripped out a garbage bag full of material, feathers, ribbons, and scraps. She shrieked and cried as she dumped the materials out all over the floor. She shook things and tossed them wildly, ripping the plastic bag in frustration.

It felt good to let herself go a little crazy. It was almost as if she left her body.

When she came back, she smoothed out the black material in front of her calmly.

She knew exactly what to do.

CHAPTER 9

At first light, the crows heard the queen's voice. She was calling from the throne.

"I have returned, come join me," she called warmly.

The crows looked at each other cautiously, but rose to heed her call.

They encircled the trees by the pond, filled with collective anxiety. They hung back, not taking the foremost branches.

Cracks did a somersault in the clearing and bonked his head on a log. He stood up and took a bow. "Don't worry, she doesn't bite. Unlike some of you folks," he said with a sly grin. "I forgive you, by the way."

The golden light reflected off the queen's soft black feathers. She gazed at them all lovingly.

"I know you have had a difficult time in my absence. And I know your hearts feel great trouble now. But I ask each one of you, for the sake of all, to take a deep look at your fear and then rise above it."

The crows were silent, unsure of what to do or say.

"You are wondering why I left you." She smiled and opened her wing to reveal Cirrus, sitting by her side. "I have brought you a prince."

The crows breathed in at the sight of the pure white little boy. To all it was a shock; to some, a horror. Crows prided themselves on being entirely black.

"What?!" shrieked the princess.

Boughbend's heart fell to see that the queen had mated.

When Cornrow had been hit by the car saving the princess as a fledgling, Boughbend had always dreamed she would choose him if she ever decided to mate again. Judging by the way Cracks gazed at the prince, Boughbend knew immediately who the father was.

What scrumptious luck, thought Lustre.

"SHE HAS MATED WITH THE KING OF THE GULLS!" he bellowed with all the ire he could muster.

"Palefeather!" "For shame!" "Lower than Low!" The crows went wild with howls.

Boughbend soared down with a warning hiss. "Kkrrrrrrlllk-kk!" He landed in front of the throne. "ENOUGH!" he shouted. "How can you welcome your queen like this? Many of you remember the ancient song of the all-white king with red eyes. It happens sometimes. This is a crow like any other."

"But his eyes are black!" protested Curbside.

"This, too, can happen," said the queen. "It is even more rare. More special. We have been blessed."

"Don't believe her lies! She has betrayed us all! She wants you to bow to the king of the gulls!" screamed Lustre, waving his wings wildly.

"Abomination!" "Palefeather!" "Betrayer!" The shrieks escalated in the trees. The energy became fiercer and more agitated.

"I AM THE FATHER!" Cracks yelled out, very seriously.

"Who can believe a fool?" asked Lustre to the group. "She is making a mockery of everything we hold dear! GET THAT LOWLY GULL!"

On his signal, thirty or so hotheaded young crows swooped

out of the trees with beaks and claws ready for blood.

"No!" shouted many others.

Boughbend and Cracks reared up to defend. The queen picked up and hurried the prince towards the Hollowing Tree. He flew as fast as he could, but it wasn't very fast.

Ruffle and several others swooped down, snatching and pecking, trying to stop the attackers from behind.

Still more of Lustre's supporters joined the fray. A mess of black scratched its way through the trees.

The queen flew evasive manoeuvres through the woods and the prince deftly mirrored her movements, staying close by her side as she flew.

Cracks's son, thought Boughbend proudly as he swiped away three oncomers with one swift claw. He hung back to defend, while Cracks flitted to gain on the queen.

Lustre rose up over the wood and soared down to the path.

The queen and her son flapped as hard as they could to cross the clearing to the Tree. Lustre gave two strong pulls and gained on them rapidly. He extended his claws within a feather's length of the prince.

Cracks zipped up into the space between them and made a silly face, saying, "*Yooo-hooo!*"

Lustre couldn't resist the urge to grab him and pin him down to the ground. With one swift peck he took out his eye.

The queen and the prince disappeared into the Hollowing Tree.

As Lustre thrust back his head to swallow the eyeball triumphantly, Cracks used the momentum to throw Lustre back on his back. Boughbend swooped in and stood over

Lustre with his talons clutched around his neck.

Cracks winked at Boughbend with his good eye to say thanks and vanished inside the hollow.

The rest of the group now hovered all around.

"I am ashamed how Low we've come," said Boughbend to the group, clenching around Lustre's neck a little tighter.

"Do it!" said Lustre from the ground. "Go ahead! Kill one of your own out of spite, mister High and mighty."

He has me by the feathers, thought Boughbend. *The queen would tell me to let him go.* He loosened the grip.

"I choose not to," said Boughbend, and he let Lustre go. "We must choose to have a broader vision," he said, remembering the girl.

"Choice! Yes," said Lustre, settling his feathers, "we all have one." He scrutinized the whole group. "If you want a king who is a crow, then meet at the playground instead of taking roost tonight."

And with that Lustre flew off, soaring as high as he could. He circled once above them all to show off the height of his flight, then veered off for the outskirts. It may have seemed dramatic, but really he just wanted to make a quick escape before anyone asked him to follow after the queen through the hollow.

Elsa was dreading the first day back at school, but everyone seemed to keep a respectful distance. Even Ms. Witherspoon had lightened up.

At recess, Eh Ta Taw kicked a soccer ball her way. "I'm glad you're back."

Elsa smiled and kicked it back to him. They played all through recess and that seemed to keep the mean girls away.

At lunch Eh Ta Taw suggested another game: trying to keep the ball aloft using anything but your hands. That was so much fun, a bunch of other kids joined in.

The day passed quickly.

It wasn't until the bell rang that Elsa felt worried. Now she wondered if Breagh, Gabby, and Lenore would try to follow her and bother her on the way home.

When she came out of the school, Claire was waiting in the car with a big smile on her face.

"The sun is shining. Let's go for a drive," she said as Elsa climbed in.

"But what about the shop?" asked Elsa.

Claire shrugged. "What can I say? I'm an artist."

They sped off for the shore, blasting tunes and singing.

When they returned from the beach, the sun was sinking. Claire took the route home through the park and stopped at the big field.

"Let's watch the sunset," said Claire.

There was an uneasy feeling as the crows hovered to take the roost. Careen waited for the princess to fly to her right, but the princess just kept circling, waiting for more and more crows who straggled in.

"Come on!" said Careen, losing her patience, "just take the whole group down to the playground."

The princess just ambled around in a circle, stalling.

"She'll favour the prince, you know. She'll probably crown him to solidify the alliance since he's a half-breed. You'll lose your place. You should just roost us all together to send a message."

"No," said the princess. "Everyone gets to make their own choice."

She chose the stand of trees along the white fence and dove down to signal to the rest of the group. Careen followed with a snarl on her face.

Once the princess had touched down to select the roost, she pushed off again. "Okay, now!" she said veering off in the direction of the playground.

Careen pushed off, surprised. Breezy didn't budge.

"I'm staying," she said.

Lustre sat atop the pinnacle of the tallest slide, feeling sorry for himself.

Only about two hundred crows had gathered to support him. As to be expected, the young hotheads had showed up, but the rest were mostly elders. *Half of them will be dead by the spring,* he thought gloomily.

There were a few decent soldiers. Wrapper and Billow, of course. Popcan was a surprise. Still, he could feel everyone's collective discomfort at the low turnout. *I could lose them all yet.*

"Make way!" shouted Careen.

The tiny group got a bit of a lift to see the princess arrive.

"You have all been brave," said Lustre doing his best to rally spirits. "And you know there are thousands more that feel as we do but just weren't brave enough to join us. Yet. We must bide our time and fly strong. They will join us in time and then we will make the park our own!"

There were just a few scattered cheers.

"Come! We'll roost across the river for now."

Lustre took lift over the water and his tiny army followed suit. Careen followed close by his side.

The princess struggled to keep up with the heights. Looking back, she could see thousands of crows circling the roost in the distance.

"I can't do it," she said. She veered back towards the park.

Careen and Lustre looked back to see her slipping away in the dimming light.

"Go with the princess," ordered Lustre.

"But—" protested Careen, feeling hurt.

It's a new world with new rules. I don't need a mate. I need a mole. "We need someone on the inside. I found the keychain. Await my message."

Careen fought back tears, but turned back dutifully.

Stupid girl, he thought.

The further Lustre flew from the park, the more he wanted it back.

Elsa and Claire stood in the field in the golden light.

Crows danced above them in the trees in their thousands. Elsa looked over at Claire.

"I'm surprised you're encouraging this."

Claire smirked and gave a little shrug. Elsa watched the crows for a while until she couldn't contain it anymore.

"Every one thinks I'm crazy, too, don't they?"

"I don't, Elsa," said Claire, looking into her eyes. Then she turned back, staring at the crows in their evening ritual, listening to their din. "This world is full of crazy things...and you just have to do your best to stay...human."

I love her. "I'm sorry I made more trouble for you," said Elsa.

Claire looked at her with that wistful smile. "I love you, Elsa. And you can stay with me forever if that's how it needs to be, okay?"

I LOVE HER! Elsa gave a little nod, so happy to have an answer at last.

They hugged each other in a way they had never been hugged.

Claire smiled a mischievous grin. "I've got something for you." She ran to the car and returned with a long, billowy, black-winged cloak. Sticks were sewn into the arms, extending the material out into great powerful wings that could be controlled by the wearer.

Elsa's jaw dropped as she pulled it on and tried it out. Her eyes filled with glee when Claire placed the crow's-head-shaped headdress on her head like a crown.

"Claire, this is incredible!" beamed Elsa.

Claire's eyes twinkled with delight as Elsa danced around her in the field, extending the wings of the costume, billowing in the wind.

"*Caw! Caw!*" called out Elsa joyously as she whirled.

Claire beamed, too.

Elsa stopped in front of her and removed the headdress crown. She placed it on Claire's head.

"You're the real queen."

"You can be my princess," said Claire, receiving the crown with a giggle.

"Nah," said Elsa picking up two branches, "Mum's the princess."

"Then who are you?"

Elsa handed her the two branches to be her wings. "I'm the jester," she smiled.

Claire laughed and extended the branches out to her sides.

They danced together happily beneath the crows, flowing and swaying in the golden light, supported by the wind.

Special thanks to Jason Rogerson, Vince and Kim Black, Htoo K'mu Paw, Wendy Poirier, Penelope Jackson, Laurie Brinklow, Terrilee Bulger, the cast and crew of the short film and of course...the crows.

Harmony Wagner is a writer, director and award-winning filmmaker based in Prince Edward Island, Canada. She has written for web, gaming, film and television including several episodes of *The Big Comfy Couch*. Her short film *Queen of the Crows* broadcast on CBC and screened at numerous festivals including Telefilm Canada's Shorts program at the Cannes Film Festival. She has directed two feature films, *Kooperman* and *Singing to Myself*. *Queen of the Crows* is her first novel.